Maybe In Monaco

Book 1 in the Monaco Series

Kaya Quinsey Holt

Maybe in Monaco
A Coco Rose Books Publication

First paperback edition 2022

978-1-7771022-4-1

For Leo—this one is for you.

Can the truth make up for a secret that runs deeper than the Mediterranean Sea?

Maybe In Monaco

ONE
Charlotte

With an old-fashioned camera teetering on the edge of the open taxi window, Charlotte Levant snapped a picture of the Monaco skyline, a haze of buildings fading into the sea and surrounding mountains. It was a warm June morning as the black Mercedes taxi sped through the winding streets.

"How long are you here for your vacation?" the taxi driver asked in a conversational tone. One of his arms dangled from the open window, which always made Charlotte nervous. Thankfully, it was impossible to become more nervous than she already was.

"Oh, I'm not actually on vacation." Charlotte's heart fluttered in her chest as the taxi swerved along the Fairmont Hairpin, an S-shaped curved road along Princess Grace Avenue. "I'm just coming back for a quick visit." *Just a quick visit*, she repeated to herself. Surely, she could handle that.

"I hope not too quick," the taxi driver said with a laugh, as he took a sharp turn and nearly clipping the car next to them. "You have family here?"

Charlotte held onto her seat as her luggage swayed. The trunk of the taxi was filled with ancient Louis Vuitton luggage, and even more was piled in the backseat beside her. "My grandmother," she said with pride. It felt strange that only her grandmother and this taxi driver knew of her homecoming. A surprising mixture of apprehension and excitement bubbled as they drew closer to their destination in the small country located in the heart of the French Riviera.

"You visit often?"

"I'm afraid not as often as I would like," Charlotte replied truthfully. She was glad that the driver hadn't asked about the last time she had come back.

He expertly wove through the paved and well-maintained streets, offering a breath-taking view of the Mediterranean Sea. It had been a long time since Charlotte passed that vista and, as the salty air wafted through the open window, she realized how much she had missed it. She snapped another photo of palm trees and cacti against the bright blue, cloudless sky as she accelerated past enchanting putty-colored buildings, Italianate architecture, and immaculately manicured hedges. A shiny Ferrari, quickly followed by an Alfa Romeo, sped past along the narrow street. Charlotte sighed as she rapped one manicured fingernail against another and tried to relax. *There was nowhere quite like home.*

The destination wasn't far from the esteemed Monte Carlo Casino, the gardens of which were in full bloom. The sun-dappled country was filled with colorful decorative turrets and terraces. The Mediterranean influence seemed to reach every corner of the country and outdoor living was evident in the prevalence of public gardens, squares, and balconies that studded each window. The entire city appeared to be celebrating, unremarkably indicating a regular day in Monaco. Placing her beloved camera back in its worn leather case, Charlotte stared out the window like she was seeing the city for the first time. In the distance, at least a dozen yachts were setting out to sea. Charlotte recognized a few of the increasingly popular mega-yachts as they shone against the azure blue water.

"So, where are you visiting from?" the taxi driver asked, turning briefly to look at her.

Charlotte smiled. "Manhattan." The driver returned his attention to the road. *New York City was another world*, Charlotte mused as the car performed a hot lap past the Monte Carlo Casino. A throng of tourists with cameras crossed in front of the taxi, slowing all of the traffic behind it. *Perhaps the two cities had some similarities*, Charlotte thought.

Today, the body of water and anonymity that protected Charlotte was 4,000 miles away.

Charlotte was a French teacher at a private school on the Upper East Side, where she put her New York University education to use. Ample time, money, and effort were spent on rebuilding her life—an accomplishment she previously thought unimaginable. What Charlotte accomplished in those ten years astonished her and her grandmother.

In Manhattan, Charlotte cultivated a refined and private image. She socialized vigilantly, and her acquaintances consisted mainly of private school colleagues. Though she scarcely noticed, Charlotte was admired and desired by many. Charlotte enticed people with her softness, attentiveness in conversations (aided by her social media avoidance), adoration for anything vintage, and passion for French impressionist art. However, Charlotte's romantic affairs were often cut short, and she developed a reputation for fleeing when relationships threatened to become too serious or prodding.

The men who courted Charlotte inevitably crashed into the walls that guarded her. Privacy was Charlotte's priority, and the less that people knew about her, the better. She feared the discovery of her imperfections, which lurked beneath every layer.

Charlotte preferred blending in to standing out. As usual, she was dressed in simple, high-quality items, which she—or her relatives—had owned for years. Her haphazardly-piled, classic travel bags were passed down from Charlotte's late mother, and her antique camera and matching leather bag belonged to her late father.

Contrary to her intention, Charlotte's subtleties spawned second glances. Strangers couldn't help noticing the authentic glamour of her well-worn Hermes handbag, slightly upturned nose, chestnut blunt cut grazing her freckled collarbones, and sparkling eyes that never gave anything away.

Slowly, Charlotte's destination crept into sight. Le Soleil was a luxury condominium with coastal views of the Côte d'Azur. Charlotte dreaded stepping out of the car, and wondered if returning was a dire mistake. "Monaco is my home," she silently repeated, as she promised herself she would.

The driver slowed to a stop, and carefully unloaded the aged Keepalls onto the unblemished cobblestone.

Charlotte remained still for a few more moments, summoning enough willpower to open the door. Once she touched her feet to the ground, the truth would land. *She was in Monaco.*

The trunk of the cab shut with a thud that rocked the whole vehicle. Taking a few deep breaths, Charlotte opened the door and set one ballet flat onto the pavement. *She was home.*

The suitcases appeared smaller and fewer to Charlotte when she left Manhattan. The driver gawked at the mountain of luggage that now blocked the sidewalk.

"That's everything," Charlotte lied, for the driver knew not of her heaviest baggage, smuggled into Monaco upon her freckle-dusted shoulders.

Charlotte paid the driver and watched as the car faded into a sea of traffic. She glanced helplessly at the unattended concierge desk and sighed. Keeping a watchful eye on her remaining belongings, Charlotte hauled her luggage into the air-conditioned lobby. She was no stranger to strenuous labor, but her arms ached and her breath grew heavier with each bag.

Ten years since she stepped foot on that cobblestone sidewalk. *Ten years* since she left the country—and the person—she loved. *Ten years* since she fled with two hearts beating inside of her. *Ten years*, and she still wondered if she made the right decision. *Ten years,* she kept a secret.

But it was very hard to keep a secret in Monaco.

TWO

Freddie

A warm breeze blew through the elegant ninth-floor Monaco apartment, which Freddie Ridgeport won in a bidding war six months earlier. Though he had paid well beyond the price he swore not to budge on, his view of the blue Mediterranean Sea and spectacular vantage of the Monaco Grand Prix each May was worth it. Located in La Condamine, a semicircle-shaped neighborhood that hugged the port, Freddie lived within walking distance to markets and world-class restaurants, and the waterfront was practically at his doorstep. After escaping a yearlong relationship with knockout Violet Macintyre, Freddie turned to his friend and former teammate, Christian, to endorse the purchase. "You'll find a cutie to share this with," Christian had assured him. *Be careful what you wish for.*

The French doors to Freddie's balcony were wide open, displaying boats of varying sizes moored along the dock and inside the harbor. The morning light poured into his opulent living room, but Freddie preferred to savor his mornings on his balcony and watch sailboats set out for adventure as the sky transitioned from pastel peach to vibrant blue.

Nicholas raced through the living room, through the adjacent kitchen and onto the balcony, nudging Freddie's lukewarm espresso off of the table in the process. With a nine year-old around, things tended to break. Freddie caught the porcelain cup mere inches before it collided with the floor.

"I might be retired, but I've still got it," Freddie boasted. He had the speed, agility, and reflexes of a professional athlete—in his case, of a recently retired Formula One driver.

"Are there any croissants?" Nicholas' voice echoed as he wandered back inside.

Freddie winced. "In the pantry," he called back. For once, Freddie had no idea what he was doing. He had accelerated from *champion* to *guardian* in record speed. Freddie, who usually thrived under pressure, was driving in the wrong lane.

The kid, as Freddie affectionately referred to him, appeared back on the balcony in pyjamas, with hair still rumpled from the night. Nicholas rubbed the sleep from his eyes. How could a kid be tired after ten hours of sleep? Freddie hadn't gotten more than five-hours, finding he was tossing and turning instead.

"Good morning. How'd you sleep?" Freddie inquired.

Nicholas shrugged and bit into his croissant, spilling crumbs haphazardly. "Okay, I guess. I had that same nightmare again."

Freddie was an expert at many things, but *kids* wasn't one of them. He wished that he could change past events, but was resentfully realizing that his abilities wouldn't always match his drive.

"Try steering to the left next time." Freddie's chest puffed up with pride as he visualized the dream that Nicholas told him about days earlier. "You said there are fields on either side, right?"

Hope appeared in Nicholas' eyes. "To the left," he repeated. "Okay. I'll try that."

Freddie rose from his seat to retrieve Nicholas' second croissant from the kitchen. They had been living together for three months, and Freddie was finally mastering the sport of caregiving. Slowly, he was learning the kid's peculiarities—from eating two croissants for breakfast every morning, to enduring frequent nightmares about car collisions. He was grateful to sneak in a little more time on his own. It's not that he disliked the company, but he had chosen to live as a bachelor. If he had wanted company, he could have had it. He liked being on his own.

"Don't forget the croissant," Nicholas bellowed from the balcony as Freddie was already halfway to the kitchen.

"Do you want that on a silver platter or a gold one?" Freddie asked dryly. *Kids.*

"Gold, please," Nicholas replied, a hint of mockery in his tone.

Six months earlier, while house hunting, Freddie's sole stipulation was location. For many years, living in Monaco had been his dream. The two hundred hectare country was the second smallest in the world, losing by a nose to Vatican City. Living in Monaco allowed Freddie to travel effortlessly within the Mediterranean, and live amongst fellow former Formula One drivers, celebrities, and billionaires. Plus, Monaco was familiar, peaceful, and relatively private. It was the perfect place for him to retire, date beautiful women, tan on beaches, have dinner at the best restaurants, and enjoy his latest hobby: boating. His retired life as an eligible bachelor had looked pretty good by his standards.

His neighborhood, La Condamine was the second-oldest neighborhood in Monaco, and Freddie adored its ceaseless aroma of salty air, freshly roasted coffee beans, and baked goods. When Formula One fans flocked each year for the Grand Prix, he could shake hands and sign autographs before conveniently returning to his private home.

His apartment had views of the sea and was adjacent to a corridor of buildings in traditional Monegasque architecture, heavily featuring granite, marble, and terracotta. Sometimes even he felt impressed on his way home after all these months. He wondered when his infatuation with the country would end, as all love affairs inevitably did.

Although it had been six-months in the apartment and three-months with Nicholas there, to him it felt like a lifetime, his old life feeling more distant by the day.

The year before, Freddie gloriously won the Monaco Grand

Prix. With three world championships and eighty podiums, the win was a spectacular end to his incredible ten-year career. Freddie was at his peak, and multiple teams were resolved to sign him. Being on top, though, meant that Freddie could only move in one direction and there was only one way for him to go: *down*. Younger and hungrier drivers were set on overtaking him. By retiring, Freddie avoided his inevitable fall from grace. If he left at his peak, he would never have to face his inevitable fall from grace.

Had retiring been a huge mistake?

He pushed the thought from his mind the same way he pushed aside boxes of gnocchi and olive tapenades. Freddie rummaged around his pantry, which was now fully stocked, proudly realizing that he was becoming a not-so-bad homeowner and legal guardian. He was keeping the kid alive. That was what parenting was all about, wasn't it? When he lived on his own, his kitchen was merely a place for takeout containers and, occasionally, preparing his signature appetizer (olives and flatbread) during the early stages of dates. Freddie never prepared a main course, preferring to continue his romantic evenings at restaurants.

He squeezed the box of viennoiseries, stuffed with croissants and pain au raisins, back into the cupboard. If Freddie had a glimpse of his future six months earlier, he might have sought an apartment with a tad more storage space.

Freddie's real estate hunt felt like a lifetime ago. Then, he merely worried about getting his beach chair close enough to the water. Pseudo-fatherhood wasn't part of the picture, or the plan. Now, his days were peppered with school drop-offs in his bright red Ferrari, and meetings with accountants. During the last three months, Freddie's brand new two-bedroom bachelor pad transformed into a family home. His formerly sleek office now housed a tiny stranger and his once-bare kitchen cupboards overflowed. In the months that Nicholas had been living with him, Freddie hadn't gone to a single restaurant. No long beach days. No yacht parties. Certainly, no day trips to Italy.

Six months earlier, everyone wanted a piece of Freddie

Ridgeport. He knew it and the world around him knew it. The world was his oyster. When he bought the place, he had just turned thirty years old. The best part: he was bound by no one after having ended his relationship with Violet Macintyre.

Violet was the type of girl Freddie wanted all of his friends—and none of his family members—to behold. Once an unnoticed high school peer, Violet had blossomed into the exemplary femme fatale. Freddie was floored by Violet's curves, unapologetic mouth, and bravado. She was the wildest ride of Freddie's romantic life, which was fitting. His previous love interests, who had been willowy, modest, well-mannered and elegant, appeared bland in comparison. But Violet's 'breath of fresh air' was secretly carbon monoxide, and Freddie found himself poisoned and suffocating. He would miss the way she looked on his arm, but Freddie already had enough trophies.

Freddie, usually wary of monogamy, initially hoped that the relationship might enable him to focus on himself. His emotional energy had previously been consumed with complex, glamorous-yet-tragic women, but Violet was different. She was the first girl with whom he could blast his father, because Violet's father was like his too. She laughed more than she cried. She allowed Freddie to indulge without restraint. Freddie eventually realized, though, that every rose has thorns.

Notoriously private Freddie was shocked to discover intimate details about himself in gossip magazines. He rarely spoke to press unless his publicity team insisted, and it didn't take long to discover that Violet was capitalizing on his musings and experiences.

Unsteady Freddie: Is Top Racer Ridgeport Saying Goodbye to F1?

Racer Ridgeport's Struggle for Acceptance as a Child

Macintyre or Mac-indecent? Star Racer Freddie Ridgeport and Girlfriend Violet Macintyre Booted from Amalfi Cathedral

Formula One or Formula for Disaster?

Freddie was thankful to have uncovered Violet's true nature before Nicholas entered the picture. When he confronted her, Violet claimed to have acted with the loving intention of maintaining his relevance. Freddie couldn't see it that way. Regardless, the aerodynamics of the relationship was wrong. The lifestyle he anticipated after ending his relationship with Violet had been brief. For a short while, single, retired, and wealthy Freddie possessed a freedom trifecta.

A few months later, a single phone call changed everything.

Freddie was confident about his strong moral compass, but his innate goodness was truly tested when he received that call from a *Philip Banks,* the alleged lawyer for the Stefano family.

"You've got to be joking," were the only words that escaped his lips during the call. He turned his phone off afterwards.

Freddie couldn't comprehend why the Stefanos appointed him sole guardianship of their only child. The Stefanos were family friends, and Nicholas, with his neat side-part and perfectly combed hair, had been his parents' pride and joy. Freddie no longer had a girlfriend or wife to act as a maternal figure, and "fatherhood" presumably did not come to mind when people thought of him. *Perhaps the Stefanos had been die hard Formula One fans?* Freddie knew only that Nicholas' parents were in their eighties and had no living relatives. It was a tragedy.

Freddie reluctantly agreed to the arrangement, having been absolutely certain, with one hundred percent confidence, that after three-months Nicholas would ask to leave. He figured this whole situation was bound to wind up in a quick call to Philip Banks, Nicholas asking to be moved to another family, and he would be the hero who gave the kid a nice place to live in the meanwhile. Freddie felt proud to enact such noble selflessness for the helpless boy. He'd teach Nicholas how to be a man, like him. However, three whole months had come and gone, and Nicholas still hadn't mentioned leaving. Freddie was becoming nervous. The kid was settling in, and damaging Freddie's office in the process by affixing photographs to the walls with thumbtacks. *Thumbtacks!*

In their short time together, Freddie struggled to bond with Nicholas. Aside from discussing his nightmares, Nicholas was withdrawn, and only left his bedroom (Freddie's office) when meals or snacks were offered. Freddie wondered what a child could do with so much time alone. *His thoughts could become sinister*, Freddie worried, recalling the creepy films Violet forced him to watch. Disturbed, evil, and possessed children were Violet's preferred horror trope. Freddie dreaded investigating, but was responsible for ensuring that the kid wasn't plotting his own death—or worse, *Freddie's*.

"Can I ask you a question?" Nicholas suddenly appeared in the kitchen with wide, searching eyes. "What was it like to drive a Formula One car?"

Freddie relaxed. *He could answer that.* "Great question. It's kind of like flying. Your heart is pumping and you're filled with energy. The car is extremely powerful. It requires a level of mastery and practice that feels almost impossible sometimes, but when you get there and feel like you're one with the car, it's completely worth it. A lot of people think that professional driving is just sitting behind a wheel, but it's so much more than that. Your entire body is involved. Every muscle contracts. It requires being in quite good shape, actually. I'm pretty good at it." Freddie couldn't help gloating when he discussed racing. It was an old habit that he did not plan on retiring.

"'Pretty good,' as in letting Theo Timsdale overtake you at Monza last year?" Nicholas replied in a thoughtful tone, as if his words weren't fire on an open wound. "Or 'pretty good,' as in crashing at the Portugal Grand Prix two seasons ago?"

Freddie glared bitterly at *the kid*, but couldn't help feeling impressed by his knowledge. "Someone's in the loop."

Nicholas smiled victoriously. "I want to race. I want to be a racecar driver. The very best."

This caught Freddie's attention. "A racecar driver? *You* want to be a racecar driver?" Freddie asked incredulously. In the months that they had spent together, Nicholas hadn't mentioned driving, racecars, or anything related to Formula One, which Freddie considered an understandable aftereffect of losing parents in a fatal car crash.

Nicholas nodded. "Who doesn't want to be a racing legend? Plus, if I'm any good at it, there will be an actual racer in this house again. One *still* on the grid."

"Please, I can lap you any day," Freddie retorted. "Come with me."

A section of Freddie's walk-in closet was devoted to his former racing gear. Freddie rummaged through his memorabilia, and presented Nicholas a small helmet.

"Try this on," Freddie instructed, his face animated. "This was my first karting helmet."

Nicholas held the helmet tentatively, and examined it from all angles. He tried fitting it onto his head, but it wouldn't budge past his ears. "Seems a bit small," he pouted.

"I was about seven when I started karting," Freddie explained. "Go-karts are how to start."

Nicholas took off the helmet, cradling it in his lap instead of handing it back. He couldn't pull his eyes away from it. "Do you think I'm too old to start?"

"At nine? No," Freddie lied. He'd have to train the kid with full commitment if he wanted a shot. "What other sports do you play?"

Nicholas kicked his feet against one another. "I don't really play sports."

Freddie's eyes widened. *What kind of kid didn't play sports?* "Not a fan?"

"No, I like sports. Ma didn't. She never wanted me to get hurt," Nicholas' pent-up grief finally spilled over. A tear slipped from his eye and landed upon his rosy cheek, which he brushed aside irately. Nicholas refused to look up, seeming frustrated with himself as he scowled.

Nicholas' divulgence conjured an emotional medley of sympathy, confusion, and trepidation in Freddie. This was the most him and the kid had talked about the situation since Nicholas had moved in three months earlier. Thank goodness for school, which Freddie had happily waved the kid off to every day. Was he equipped to raise this child?

"I guess this is my new home though." Nicholas looked around the apartment as if he was seeing it for the first time. "You sure like grey, huh?"

"Grey's nice. It goes with everything," Freddie said, looking around.

Nicholas shrugged. "Sure could use a bit of color..."

Freddie tried to change the subject. He hardly wanted the kid to start re-arranging things. "I get it, kid. Look, you moving in here is what your parents wanted, but if you're not happy—"

"It's fine here. My parents always rooted for you when you were racing on TV. It was the only sport we watched." Nicholas ran his fingers over the too-small racing helmet. "And you let me order the food I want."

It's fine here. Freddie was conflictingly proud and apprehensive of Nicholas' validation. He won over Nicholas, but conceivably lost his solitude in the process. Why did Freddie *have* to succeed, even when he didn't want the reward? He liked Nicholas, but he wasn't a father.

Nicholas ran his fingers over the too-small racing helmet.

"So just to check... you've got no aunts? No uncles? Is there anyone else who you might want to try living with instead?" Freddie inquired, his voice uncharacteristically fragile.

Nicholas shook his head with resolve. "Nope."

"Nope?" Freddie echoed.

"It was just us. Ma and Father were older. They were eighty, which is nearly one hundred. They explained it to me last year when I turned eight. There's no aunts or uncles or other grown ups really."

Freddie's heart sunk. Did that mean that the kid was really, seriously and truly thinking of...staying? He liked Nicholas, sure, but he wasn't exactly a father-figure. He barely knew the kid! *Nah, this wasn't going to really happen. Nicholas will want to leave.* He repeated that to himself through strained breaths.

"Well this has been quite the talk, Nicholas. Do you want me to call you that: Nicholas? Or Nick?"

"Nicholas is fine."

"All right, Nicholas. I'm glad we had this talk. Maybe we could talk about some things later," Freddie said. Later, he planned to suggest hiring a counsellor for Nicholas to speak to. Freddie checked his watch. "Hey, don't you have school or something to get to?"

Nicholas wrinkled his nose. "It's the weekend. We don't have classes on the weekend."

Freddie's attention veered. Through the window, he was struck by the bewildering sight of a woman walking along the sidewalk, who bore striking resemblance to someone he thought about often, never spoke of, and had reconciled himself to never seeing again. *That graceful walk. That hazelnut hair. Could it really be Charlotte Levant?* He ran to the edge of the balcony to get a closer look.

"What are you looking at?" Nicholas asked, following him and peering over the railing to the street below.

Freddie shook his head as the woman turned a corner and disappeared from sight. "Just my imagination," he said with an uneasy laugh. If he had been in a forthcoming mood, or had perhaps been a poet instead of a racecar driver, Freddie might have told Nicholas that he swore he saw the only woman he ever loved. Charlotte Levant disappeared from Monaco ten years ago, without even saying "goodbye."

Freddie willed back his rationality, chastising himself for being so ridiculous. Having *the kid* in the house was uprooting memories that Freddie had suppressed. His mind was playing tricks on him. But given the tiniest chance that it *had* been Charlotte, Freddie would never forgive himself for missing the opportunity.

"Grab your jacket," he shouted.

"Where are we going?"

"To the track," Freddie heard himself saying.

Nicholas eagerly ran to his room, kicking off his slippers along the way. Within moments, Freddie heard the kid call "ready!" from the front door.

Freddie made decisions the same way he drove: swiftly, determinedly, and unwaveringly. He had mastered the Circuit de Monaco, so he could handle being stuck at a crossroads. Regardless, it was a weekend and Freddie was retired. He had nothing to lose and everything to gain.

THREE
Charlotte

Charlotte knocked on the updated dark wood door at the end of the hallway. A flurry of memories and emotions washed over her. She always knew that she would have to return to Monaco, but it still felt too soon. She gripped the brass door knocker. The last time Charlotte was here, she was seeking help from her mémé and, today, the roles were reversed.

She drew an inward breath and the door swung upon, revealing Marguerite, draped in a linen robe. Her chestnut hair, which matched Charlotte's, was fastened in a mussed chignon with a clip. Tears sprung to Charlotte's eyes immediately. *Her mémé.*

"Charlotte. *Mon cherie*," Marguerite said in her familiar warm-yet-formal tone.

"Mémé," Charlotte greeted her grandmother with the manners she'd taught her, kissing one cheek, then the other.

"Now, let me have a look at you," Marguerite turned Charlotte from side to side. "*Bonne*," she declared. "You may come in."

Charlotte studied her mémé's face, which had aged only slightly throughout the decade. Marguerite's eyes still sparkled, and her decline was evident solely by the shadows beneath them. Marguerite's physique, however, was noticeably fragile.

"Come give your mémé a hug. I won't break. I'm not frail." Marguerite offered an embrace with one arm and clutched her cane with the other.

Three months earlier, Marguerite fell and fractured her hip after enjoying the best ratatouille in the Riviera. Not wanting to worry Charlotte, she underwent surgery privately and alone, and informed Charlotte only one week ago. Charlotte was horrified that her mémé, now recovering resiliently, had kept such news from her. Devastated to be so far away, Charlotte purchased a one-way plane ticket.

Dependable Charlotte (or "Ms. Levant," as her students called her) never called in sick, took vacations, or required accommodation. Her career had become her purpose, identity, and essential distraction from unfriendly thoughts. In this situation, though, work was irrelevant. Citing a family emergency, Charlotte formally requested a leave of absence, but her flight was already booked. Charlotte was going to Monaco—and she dreaded it.

Charlotte wrapped her mémé in a hug, and the familiar bergamot and tuberose notes of Creed *Fleurissimo* engulfed her.

"I'm sorry I waited so long," Charlotte whispered, concern audible in her voice.

"My dear, one mustn't apologize," Marguerite insisted.

"How are you? How is the pain? Are you feeling alright?"

Marguerite laughed and waved Charlotte off. "The doctors have me on more pain medication than you could imagine. *Cherie*, please, I don't like to make a fuss." She turned back to the living room and placed herself delicately onto the tufted white leather sofa. Charlotte hated witnessing her mémé, who once glided so effortlessly, wince as she lowered herself onto the couch.

Years ago, Charlotte believed that the apartment would be her home forever. Her mémé was all Charlotte had left.

Marguerite's Rosa Aurora marble floors led to a panoramic view of the Mediterranean Sea, visible through the corner apartment's glass walls. The luxurious home, filled with 19th century porcelain vases that her mémé had long collected, induced a tsunami of memories. Marguerite had beautifully maintained the antique Baccarat crystal chandelier, which teenage Charlotte nearly smashed with a Jules René

Hervé painting while moving in. Her childhood memories of Marguerite were scarce before then.

Charlotte's parents were two of the many people she tried desperately to not think about. She was only sixteen years old when they passed away.

"Who would have thought, after all these years, you would come back?" Marguerite mused.

"When I left, I didn't think I'd be gone so long," Charlotte answered, forcing a laugh. "I shouldn't have waited." If Charlotte knew how long she would miss Monaco and her mémé, she might have never left in the first place. Then again, Charlotte *had* to leave. She would have withered amongst the secrets and the constant reminders of those she had lost.

"You have your mother's wanderlust," Marguerite remarked with a wry smile.

Charlotte's relationships were complex with both parents before their deaths, so she took comfort in Marguerite's simplicity and emotional stability. When she moved in, she felt—for the first time—that someone was watching out for her.

The two years in that apartment were the most complicated of Charlotte's life, filled with the highest of highs and lowest of lows. She recalled asking why her mémé hadn't played a larger role in her life until then, and learned that the family business had taken precedence. Marguerite had been immersed in building the Levant Yachting empire with Charlotte's grandfather. It was the most exciting endeavor of Marguerite's life, but the long hours and frequent traveling cut into her time with her only son and grandchild. Marguerite had promised to make up for her infrequent presence during Charlotte's childhood, and she certainly kept that promise. Now, it was Charlotte's turn to apologize for squandered time.

"I've missed you and the sun so much. I really missed Monaco." Charlotte paced through the familiar home, marveling at the expansive views. Golden light formed a dappled pattern on the marble floor, and Charlotte could hear the faint hubbub from the streets below.

Manhattan had become Charlotte's haven, chance to rebuild, and safe place. Still, she had grown weary of the cold weather that accounted for seemingly half of each year. Grey, overcast days were difficult to power through while simultaneously battling an internal storm. It seemed far easier to be happy when the sun was shining, as it did throughout most days in Monaco.

"I recognize so much of myself in you, Charlotte," Marguerite said. "I needed to build a life of my own at that age too." She carefully reached for her cup of tea, and her hand trembled slightly.

Charlotte lived by a motto that Marguerite taught her: "If you keep things light and shiny, your emotions will be tidy." She veered the conversation towards the framed photographs mounted in Marguerite's kitchen. Snapshots of Charlotte and Marguerite at the Monaco Grand Prix and the South of France dangled amid portraits of New York City that Charlotte had taken.

She bit into one of the pistachio macarons her meme had left out and withheld an inward moan as the delicate crunch of the shell led to a silky, sweet filling. That bite alone was worth Charlotte's entire journey.

Marguerite's shrine to their relationship illuminated Charlotte's guilt. Charlotte had worried extensively about her return's impact on herself, but hardly considered her absence's impact on her mémé.

Marguerite always held her chin high, had exciting plans for the future, and *never* surrendered to sadness. Even when Marguerite's son died, thrusting her into the role of caring for a teenager, she persisted with gusto. Like her apartment, Marguerite shone radiantly.

"Tell me, is there a man in New York? Is that why you stayed in America so long? You can dodge the subject on the telephone, but you can't hide from me here," her mémé pried, her eyes dancing.

Charlotte bit down a smile. Each time they spoke, Marguerite asked the same question, and Charlotte gave the same answer. Marguerite feigned forgetfulness, but Charlotte knew that her grandmother was a huge—and nosy—romantic.

"No, mémé. Like I keep telling you, I don't want a boyfriend right now. I'm here to focus on you!" Charlotte was *mostly* telling the truth, because what good could come from admitting that she hid from love behind walls far less shiny than the rosy marble Marguerite was accustomed to?

Marguerite rested her eyes, and the corners of her lips tipped upwards serenely. "You can't blame me for asking, and I don't need help. Are you happy with your life, Charlotte?"

"I am happy," Charlotte asserted as convincingly as possible. A creeping feeling of unsettlement caused her to fuss with her battered cuticles. If her voice hadn't exposed her agitation, her fingernails had. "I'm certainly happy to see you." At least *that* part was true.

"Your return was well-timed, Charlotte. I've been avoiding sharing some news with you. I couldn't tell, by your voice alone, if you were sturdy enough to receive it." Marguerite noticed Charlotte's panicked expression and added, "It isn't about me."

"Who died?" Charlotte asked, her throat constricting. She'd been down this road before.

Marguerite averted her pained gaze. "The Stefanos. Roland and Isabelle. It was a car accident. Three months ago. Apparently, it was quick and they didn't suffer."

Charlotte's pulse quickened. Her mouth turned dry and heat prickled her skin. She searched her mémé's face for more information. "And the son?" Charlotte finally managed. The words shot from her mouth in an agitated and desperate roar.

"I don't know details, but he wasn't involved in the accident."

Charlotte wanted to scream. Her bloodline was cursed. *The Stefanos couldn't be dead.*

"Where is he?" Charlotte implored, her voice stretching two octaves higher than usual. Charlotte's accelerating terror was undoubtedly audible as it labored within her, threatening to rupture and reveal what she had kept hidden.

"I'm not sure," Marguerite responded apologetically.

Charlotte was barely listening now. "Nine years old is far too young to lose your parents," she muttered. Charlotte, too, had lost her parents young, but not *that* young. She shook her head vigorously to expel her imagination's composite drawings of the boy—*her* boy. Her hands trembled. "Nine-years-old." She let out a guttural shudder as a single tear fell from her eye onto her hand, which she rubbed into her skin in soothing motions.

This wasn't the first time that the child had lost his parents. The nine year-old boy lost his biological parents at birth, including one with no knowledge of his existence. Only Charlotte, Marguerite, and a very discreet lawyer knew the unspoken truth. And of course the Stefanos.

"What's going to happen to him?" Charlotte whispered.

Her mémé shook her head and placed a steady hand on Charlotte's shaking shoulders. "I'm not sure, *mon cherie*, I'm not sure."

Charlotte and Marguerite lapsed into silence as Charlotte catastrophized. Her eyes narrowed as she looked upon the street below, the expansive sea, and the fleet of boats docked in front of Le Soleil. *That young boy could be anywhere. He could be on one of those boats.*

Charlotte understood that she had forfeited her legal rights to be a mother, but that was conditional upon her child living in a safe, healthy, and happy home. It was now Charlotte's responsibility to lighten, shine, and tidy the situation. First, she would need that lawyer.

"The lawyer—" Charlotte began, jumping to her feet.

"Pass my phonebook."

Marguerite's indigo Montblanc diary extensively recorded contact information for every person she had ever met. Some pretty impressive names were listed in that book, but Charlotte only cared about one. Charlotte gnawed two fingernails while her mémé skimmed through the non-alphabetized names.

Charlotte's seemingly-picturesque upbringing had trained her in the art of remaining reasonably composed under pressure. Growing up in the South of France with her French father and Canadian mother, things were rarely as they appeared. As a result, Charlotte learned to discount first impressions.

Charlotte's late mother, Octavia Levant (née Graham), suffered from undiagnosed depression throughout most of her adult life. At her core, Octavia ached, but she was brilliantly intoxicating upon first impression and commanded the attention of many. At the age of nineteen, Octavia met Charles Levant, a handsome and successful French businessman ten years her senior, while he was in Montreal on business. After a whirlwind romance and proposal, Octavia found herself more depressed than ever, isolated in a new country without nearby friends or family.

As a child, Charlotte sensed that her mother was *different.* Despite her helpless efforts to protect Octavia from the melancholic monster that tormented their family, Charlotte lost her mother to suicide. Charlotte suspected a curse when her father died one year later, scuba diving off the coast of Italy.

At sixteen, Charlotte became an orphan—although, one could argue that she'd always been one. Scarcely parented, the emotional burdens of the Levant household fell upon Charlotte's tiny shoulders—until her mémé swooped in to become both the mother and father Charlotte desperately needed. No novice to tragedy, teenage Charlotte trudged through with stoicism. Only Marguerite witnessed the looming trauma that bubbled beneath the surface of Charlotte's thick skin. That year, after moving from the family estate in Saint-Jean-Cap-Ferrat to Le Soleil in Monaco, Charlotte met Freddie.

"Philip Banks." Marguerite handed Charlotte the phonebook, reminding Charlotte of the moment she received her key to the home twelve years earlier.

"Thank you," Charlotte breathed, kissing her mémé's cheek gratefully. She picked up the landline receiver and popped a rose-flavored macaron into her dry mouth.

Amidst uncertainty, Charlotte clung to the dependable—her mémé and macarons.

FOUR
Marguerite

The word "independent" perfectly described Marguerite Levant. Metal screws, plates, and a rod held her right side in place, but Marguerite's Monaco apartment remained spotless. With her ebony and silver cane, she glided gracefully around the exquisite, hand-picked treasures that comprised the home. Marguerite, the tenacious nurturer of the dwelling she'd so scrupulously cultivated, considered outsourcing abominable. Who would *pay* another person to swindle their most cherished and therapeutic moments? Domestic "help" was reserved for unsentimental undertakings. Marguerite's hairstylist, for example, was invited to maintain her weekly blowouts.

Marguerite's 72-year-old sea green eyes still sparkled, with or without her heavy dose of pain medication. They sparkled especially brightly today. Her *chérie* was finally home.

Marguerite poured French Earl Grey into two teacups as Charlotte concluded her conversation with Philip Banks.

For Marguerite, Monaco was home. Nothing topped strolling past the palatial Hotel Hermitage in the Square Beaumarchais. The neoclassical Belle Epoque building did more for her than architecture she could imagine elsewhere. Was there any other museum as stunning as the Oceanographic Museum? A masterpiece built into the face of a cliff, it enriched her soul as much as it fed her mind. Passing by the Prince's Palace whenever she visited Monaco's Old Town left her awe-struck each and every time. The whole country, filled with pastel-colored buildings, was sun-kissed and never burnt. Why would she ever want to go anywhere else?

She understood why Charlotte had needed to leave, but she could never imagine leaving that country herself. Monaco had been her home for nearly fifty years. Since her late twenties, and even well before then, it was her home away from home. Saint-Maxime, the nearby beach town located on the Côte d'Azur in the South of France, was where she was born and raised. Marguerite had come to Monaco for her late husband's business nearly fifty years ago and stayed. It was the Stefanos, another young couple a few years their senior, who had made Monaco feel so welcoming. Her family had watched with wide eyes as their business grew and succeeded beyond their wildest dreams. No one could have guessed that a yacht chartering business would ever be as prosperous as it was.

Although she now lived alone, she didn't desire a companion. At least, not of the male variety. A nice small dog was on her thoughts lately. But she didn't need another husband or boyfriend to keep her company. She had already had the greatest love affair in what she believed to be the history of the world. She wished more than anything that Charlotte could have it easier in that regard. Marriage certainly wasn't easy but at least she hadn't had trouble finding the right person.

Marguerite knew better than to ask questions. Instead, she patted the seat next to her.

Charlotte sat down, carefully balancing her head on her Marguerite's lean shoulder. "Can you tell me a story?"

"What kind?" Marguerite smiled, for she already knew the answer.

"A love story."

Marguerite stroked her granddaughter's hair in a soothing fashion. "It all began in the summer of 1961…"

Marguerite had never heard a better love story than her own.

Charlotte's late grandfather, Luc Levant, was her grandest luxury. Though they both grew up in Sainte-Maxime, their roads didn't cross until Marguerite reached the precocious age of sixteen. By then, she was leggy, tanned, an aspiring model, and an accounting assistant for her father's marine mechanics company. At an open call for an emerging brand in Saint-Tropez, Marguerite was enchanted by the eighteen year-old young man behind the camera. The intensity of their immediate connection was captured in the photographs.

Luc was chastised for misusing time and film during Marguerite's audition, but still managed to catch Marguerite before she left. Of course, Marguerite had intentionally lingered, certain that Luc would pursue her. The following evening, she and Luc dined on mussels and house red wine at a simple brasserie. They exchanged stories about their upbringing, and Marguerite divulged her experience and passion for accounting. Although she knew and cared little for the intricacies of boats, Marguerite understood numbers. Luc was enraptured. Marguerite, too, became lost in the intensity of Luc's blue eyes and with which he spoke.

Luc enjoyed photography, but was ultimately planning to create his own business. He had grand ambitions and dreams, and was looking for the right woman to help him. Marguerite knew that she was that woman.

"It reminds me of my first date with Freddie," Charlotte quietly interrupted. She hugged her knees against her chest.

"Then came the wedding," Marguerite continued.

Two years after their first date, Marguerite was eighteen and married to Luc. Luc was twenty and his ambition had soared. With Marguerite's father as his mentor, Luc was determined to start a yacht chartering business out of Monaco. He was a natural entrepreneur who jumped wholeheartedly into everything—be it photography, business, or love-making.

Taking a loan to start the business was a dicey move, but Marguerite couldn't bear squashing her husband's excitement when he obtained pre-approval to finance a pre-owned yacht. She stood by

Luc's side, running the company's numbers. By her twenty-first birthday, Marguerite was bouncing a newborn baby on her lap while operating the financials for Levant Yachting in Sainte-Maxime. Marguerite's father retired his marine mechanic career to assist his only daughter and son-in-law with the intricate boat work, saving the couple from paying other experts.

The company's first yacht, *La Reve ("The Dream")* was Marguerite and Luc's pride and joy—aside from their brand-new baby, Charles, of course.

"I can't believe you weren't stressed," Charlotte marveled.

Marguerite threw her head back and laughed. "*Mon cherie*, I was stressed all the time. I was also incredibly, inexplicably content. I felt alive every single day."

When Marguerite's father died, her connections and social network in the South of France shrunk considerably. Her childhood friends were busy with their own lives, and her extended family members were scattered in towns along the Riviera. She leaned on Luc for support more than ever, and their fondness for one another grew as they nurtured the business and baby intertwined. The pair became great friends in addition to newlyweds.

As Marguerite predicted, Levant Yachting began generating profit within its first two years. Luc dreamed of buying a property in Monaco and moving the business, but Marguerite determined that they were still eons away from that achievement. Instead, the couple made upgrades to *La Reve,* and relocated to a rented apartment in Monaco that boasted a fancier address—but was smaller—than their home in Sainte-Maxime. To Luc, this was a step in the right direction, but it took Marguerite some time to reach the same conclusion. Marguerite was consistently cautious, while Luc wasn't burdened by a single doubt.

"It was your grandfather's dream," Marguerite emphasized to her granddaughter. "Relationships are all about give and take. Sometimes, all you need is a little bit of trust and faith."

Savvy Marguerite kept an eye on aviation trends as air travel became increasingly affordable and commonplace. Following Prince Rainier's marriage to Grace Kelly, Monaco became the embodiment of prestige, and tourists flocked to the small Riviera country to brush shoulders with the elite. Levant Yachting's desired clientele included tourists craving a few hours of Monaco-style grandeur, and business owners striving to impress their own clients and stakeholders. Levant Yachting boomed as Monaco's political tensions dissipated, and the Monaco Grand Prix gained popularity around the globe.

Despite her success as a businesswoman, wife, and mother, Marguerite felt homesick, and often longed for the familiar faces of Sainte-Maxime. Marguerite grew uncharacteristically lonesome—until the *Stefanos* changed everything. Roland and Isabelle Stefano were a married couple, around a decade older than Luc and Marguerite. Luc met Roland at Monaco's port, where Roland owned and operated a successful import-export company. Luc and Roland practically lived at the yacht club during those days, making new connections and learning about the intricacies of business in Monaco. Roland offered Luc invaluable advice about succeeding in the small country, and the two became immediate friends.

Marguerite got along splendidly with Roland's wife, Isabelle. Marguerite desired female friendship during those lonely days as a new mother and businesswoman, and Isabelle filled that void. Isabelle, who longed for a child, was similarly fulfilled by helping to care for Charles. Isabelle confided to Marguerite that she and Roland were unable to have children, and Roland was reluctant to adopt. Roland and Isabelle soon became Charles' surrogate uncle and aunt.

At a point in Luc and Roland's friendship, Levant Yachting's business slowed, and Luc worried that the company's money would not tide his family over for the upcoming season. He confided in Roland that he could no longer afford his Monaco apartment, and was contemplating moving back to France. Roland wouldn't hear of it. He immediately whipped out his checkbook and wrote the Levants a loan. Luc would never have accepted a loan from anyone else, but Roland had become family. Business picked up, and Luc paid Roland back within the year. Soon after, Luc and Marguerite bought their Le Soleil apartment, and they never looked back.

On the Riviera, excess was everywhere. It dripped from wrists and floated under pedicured feet. For the first time in Marguerite's life, it saturated her world too.

Over the years, Charles grew to be just like his father and was a genius in business. Watching his father edge out the competition and grow his yacht fleet from one, to two, to ten had proven to be the best business education anyone could have received. As Charles grew from his infancy to childhood to teenage-years, he helped with the business in his spare time. Eventually, Charles was in his thirties himself and a business tycoon in his own right—working as the CEO of a large hotel chain that was steadily growing through the French Riviera. He hadn't followed in his father's footsteps with the family business, but it was just as well. Marguerite knew how to manage Luc, and there really was only room for one Levant man at the head of that company.

Money was never the goal for Marguerite and Luc, although it certainly didn't hurt. Luc seemed motivated to accomplish whatever seemed impossible, even into his fifties with a fully-grown child and granddaughter on the way. Marguerite's ability to manage the finances and find loopholes kept them one step ahead of the competition for decades. They were always a team. As the two of them got older, they received numerous offers to buy out the business. Selling was never an option.

"Even though I really never knew grandfather, seeing those boats always made me feel connected to him in some way."

Marguerite reached over and placed her hand on Charlotte's before continuing. "I'm glad you feel that way. Your grandfather would have loved to hear that. I suppose that's the love story you asked for."

"I like your stories," Charlotte said, looking out the window. "Can you tell me some more?"

"Oh, I don't know about that," Marguerite said dismissively. "I think we've had more than enough for one day."

"Please? How about how my parents met? I really don't know

much about their lives before me. Even then, I didn't know much about their lives."

Marguerite sighed. "All right. You're sure?"

Charlotte nodded.

"Well, speaking of your grandfather..." Marguerite picked up where she left off.

Luc had died suddenly of a heart attack on the putting green. At 56, Marguerite was a widow. No one had expected it. This was when another chapter of their lives was supposed to have begun. They had an adult son to bond with, a daughter-in-law who seemed like she could use some support, and a new-born granddaughter—their only grandchild—Charlotte. These were supposed to have been the golden years. To Marguerite, it was a devastating shock that left her shaken for months, if not years. Some mornings, she still awoke in a half-daze expecting Luc to be there beside her. But the other side of the bed was always empty. She had taken to sleeping in the middle of the bed now.

When Luc had died, her son Charles had stepped up to the plate, offering his distraught mother comfort. Meanwhile, he appeared to be doing his best to survive the loss himself. Lost in a sea of confusion, Charles expressed to her that he wished he had his father back. He said he needed his father's advice, strength, wisdom, and that sense of unwavering confidence that he had always admired. Marguerite had wanly smiled, wishing she could offer that same support. But there was no replacement for a father.

That first year without Luc Levant was undeniably tough. Although her son had been raised in Monaco and adored the small country, she had revered watching him grow and find his own niche. Her son had found financial success as the CEO of Marque, the growing hotel chain. He appeared eager to make a name for himself and inspired by the grit of his parents (he had told her over dinner once and she had never forgotten those words), Charles told her that he hadn't wanted to merely take over his family business. He had wanted success all on his own. Marguerite understood and luckily so had her husband when he was alive. Luc had never once pushed their son to take over, something which he had confided to Marguerite that he both respected and felt hurt by. It had all seemed to work out for Charles though, despite his relationship misgivings.

Early on in his career at the tender age of twenty-one, when he was still a sales strategist at Marque, Marguerite had kissed her son goodbye as he left to visit Montreal for a conference. It was where he had met eighteen-year-old Octavia Graham. Octavia was gorgeous, bubbly, and confessed that she was desperate to see the world. After what appeared to be a whirlwind romance and even wilder wedding, Charles left Canada a month later with a wife. Marguerite had never been one for convention and hadn't minded that her son had eloped but it was the speed at which their relationship moved that worried her. She knew that initial spark was better than almost anything on earth; but when the work-days were long, the demands of life piling up, and time together dwindling, marriage could inevitably be hard. It took more than merely attraction to make things work. Marguerite had desperately hoped her son knew that.

It became clear to everyone, especially Marguerite, that Octavia struggled with being away from her family. Often sullen, she also struggled to make friends with locals due to the language barrier...Octavia had come from an Anglophone part of Montreal. It hadn't helped that Charles was often away for work and Marguerite and Luc were, at the time, fully immersed in their business venture. Isolated and seemingly falling into a deeper depression, Octavia struggled even further with the challenges that motherhood provided. Marguerite would have done so much differently if she had the chance.

"It was a different time," Marguerite said, trying to explain.

Charlotte frowned. "I didn't know all that about mom."

"I think she would have done things differently too. Again, things were different back then. We didn't meddle in people's emotional lives. Perhaps we should have."

Marguerite knew that Charles felt a crushing weight of guilt as the years passed; his wife becoming sicker and his only daughter becoming increasingly independent—not due to choice. Like his father, Charles was addicted to his work. Although he saw the impact that it had on his loved ones, there was always the infallible belief that if he came through on a project, worked harder, and got the deal done, that everything would somehow work itself out. In business, that had been true. But fifteen years after his father died, Charles found himself grieving again. This time, it was the loss of his wife. It was devastating and shocking when Charles learned that Octavia drove her car off of a winding road and into a tree. She appeared to be sick. He knew that without question. But had he really been that blind to her suffering?

During the years since Luc had passed, it seemed that she had become increasingly close with her only son. He had even gone so far as to buy a family estate in Saint-Jean-Cap-Ferrat, which was just a short drive from Monaco. In hindsight, nothing made sense. It could have been a beautiful life. After all, her son had made the money, bought the house, achieved objective fiscal and business success, and had a poised and responsible adolescent daughter who gave them no grief. It was a magnificent life, or so Marguerite had thought of her son. That year, when Charlotte was fifteen, Charles had confided in her that he thought it best that Charlotte spend more time in Monaco. According to her son, Charlotte needed a stable female presence and he couldn't think of a single person better to suit that role than Marguerite.

Equal parts happy to spend time with her granddaughter and equal parts shame had engulfed her. She had felt awful thinking she didn't know her own granddaughter as well as she would have liked at the time, and equal parts frustrated with her son for pawning off responsibilities onto her.

"That's where our story really picked up," Marguerite said, her face illuminating like the sun over the sea.

"A sad beginning. Hopefully a happier ending," Charlotte said with a wry grin.

Marguerite had welcomed her granddaughter to Le Soleil with trepidation. She had never raised a daughter. She had done her best with her son, but look how that had turned out? Truthfully, Marguerite had been petrified of making a mistake. She was never going to let her granddaughter know that though. Her granddaughter needed structure. She needed stability. She needed something different than what she had received all those years. Marguerite had no idea how she would go about providing that, but she thought it was at least worth a shot.

Although the arrangement had been for Charlotte to attend her final two years of high school in Monaco, and spend time at the apartment afterwards, it turned out that Charlotte spent the majority of her time with her grandmother. Marguerite was at once elated to spend time with her granddaughter, who seemed shrouded in mystery. She wanted to chastise her son for not paying greater attention to his family, but it was evident that Charles was hurting after the loss of Octavia. It would have done no one any good for her to speak her mind, and after being married to Luc for decades, Marguerite had learned that when it came to important conversations, timing was everything.

It was important Charlotte had come to her when she had. One year later, loss hit the Levant family once again—this time, in the form of a scuba diving accident. Charles Levant was sorely missed by his mother and daughter. At that point, Marguerite and Charlotte felt almost numb upon hearing the news. Their bodies defense mechanism to buffer the pain they had both felt so acutely in the past was in full swing. That numbness seemed more dangerous in a fifteen year old, but Marguerite did the best she could. They made due in Le Soleil and Monaco became both of their homes.

"Here we are, ten years later," Marguerite declared. "Have I told you how happy I am to have you back?"

"Yes," Charlotte said. "I gathered as much."

"Good," Marguerite said with a wink. "Now, why don't you put on another pot of tea and you can tell me how that phone call went with Philip Banks? Or do you not want to talk about it?"

Charlotte took a deep breath before standing. "Good idea. I'll make a pot of tea. Yes, I'm ready to talk about it. Somehow, I think it might make things feel a bit easier."

Charlotte went to fix another pot of tea. For Marguerite, the memory of having a fifteen-year-old Charlotte coming to stay with her brought the same butterflies as it did now. Although Charlotte was now twenty-eight, she felt the same maternal protectiveness that she had felt about her only grandchild years earlier when Charlotte had needed her and she had needed Charlotte. Her granddaughter was the light in her life when she needed it most—when she had lost her husband, then her daughter-in-law and son. Charlotte had brought the sunshine back to Monaco, or at least back into Marguerite's apartment. Her granddaughter was her savior and she desperately needed a dose of brightness now. What Marguerite hadn't known was how much she had saved her granddaughter in turn. Of course, that all happened before Charlotte's secret. That secret which had been the source of horror, joy, and later sorrow for the two of them, but mostly for Charlotte.

Charlotte had needed her back then. And particularly now that it was ten years later, Marguerite had no clue just how much she needed Charlotte or how much Charlotte needed her right now. Marguerite sipped at her herbal tea as she sat in her chair, the same chair she had sat at for three months, wondering if and when she would ever see her beloved granddaughter again. Hating to be a burden, she hadn't wanted to plead for Charlotte to return. What if she had said no? That paralyzing fear had kept her quiet for months. But if she had only known that a broken hip had gotten her granddaughter back, she would have done it again years sooner.

FIVE
Freddie

Freddie took the long route to the karting track, hoping to catch another glimpse of the woman he spotted from his balcony. His former teammate and fellow retired Formula One racer, Christian Driver, had grown up in the Riviera, and recommended MonacoGo for Nicholas. Christian insisted on meeting the two of them there.

Freddie had always envied Christian's surname, which gave him edge. Like him, Christian started with go-karting, and worked his way up through the Junior Monaco Kart Cup, Formula 4, Formula 3, and Formula 2.

Nicholas' determination worried Freddie. Racing wasn't for everyone. Nicholas had been through a lot in the past few months and Freddie wasn't sure how he might withstand failure. Regardless, Freddie would provide his best coaching—when to brake, accelerate, or pass, and how to manage an adrenaline rush.

Freddie and Nicholas got in for free—not that it mattered. The wealthier Freddie became, the less he paid for. Freddie recognized the irony. A fan asked Freddie for his autograph, and he obliged with a lopsided grin and a wink. Freddie dominated this world. The course was for children, but the sound of motors revving still fueled him.

"You're sure you want to do this?" Freddie asked as he helped Nicholas suit up. If Nicholas was to be seen with Freddie, expectations would be huge.

"I'm sure," Nicholas asserted. His eyes appeared wide and alert, fixated solely on the circuit ahead.

"Just in time," Freddie announced, as Christian strutted towards them. Children and their parents crowded around the celebrity duo, but Nicholas didn't flinch.

"Nicholas, my man, the future Formula One legend!" Christian's strikingly white teeth contrasted against his deeply tanned skin. Christian possessed a charismatic warmth that made people fall in love. He made people feel amazing. What's more—it was genuine. But on the track, Christian was vicious and did whatever it took to win. He was Freddie's worst enemy on the track, and best friend off of it.

Christian had retired two years earlier than Freddie and had an apartment with his wife in Nice. His friend preferred the large French city to Monaco. Now, he spent his time gambling and investing his money simultaneously and had begun sailing in his spare time. In his last year of racing, he had married his high school sweetheart, Berta. Freddie had never had a sister, but if he had, he would have wanted her to be like Berta. Although Christian was married, he was Freddie's eternal wingman right up until Freddie had become a guardian. Christian, who didn't want children and neither did Berta, had been stunned when Freddie announced he was going to give being a guardian a shot. Freddie hadn't seen his friend in the last few months and it was the first time Christian and Nicholas were meeting.

"Christian Driver," Nicholas murmured in awe. "You're Christian Driver."

Freddie laughed lightly. He hadn't told Nicholas that Christian would be meeting them. He assumed Christian would show up while *the kid* was on the track. As always, though, Christian arrived faster than expected.

"Christian is a good friend of mine," Freddie explained to Nicholas.

Nicholas was starstruck as he gazed at Christian from beneath his tiny helmet and neck brace. "You're my favorite driver in the world. Seriously. I can't think of anyone else who compares."

Christian burst out laughing as Freddie bristled. "Don't worry, Fred. I'm sure you're in his top ten," Christian teased. He squatted to Nicholas' height, and gave the same advice as Freddie. This time, Nicholas hung onto every word.

"To warm up, the first thing you'll do is a *formation lap*," Christian explained. "The goal is to get a feeling for the grid."

"You ready?" Freddie asked. The grid was packed with kids who could have been racing for years. He hoped that Nicholas would enjoy the ride, even if he was lapped. For reasons unknown to him, Freddie's heart thumped jarringly and his brow furrowed. "Just take it one lap at a time. And whatever you do, have fun!" Freddie knew that his words meant nothing. He recognized the look on *the kid's* face—Nicholas was there to win. Freddie had that same look when he wanted something.

It was go-time.

"You'll do great," Christian called loudly enough from the sideline to be heard above the engines' roars. Nicholas nodded towards him and fixed his eyes on the grid.

Freddie turned to his friend. "And that's Nicholas," he laughed. "Welcome to my new life."

"He's a mini *you*," Christian marveled. "Have you looked at him?"

Freddie frowned. "He is not." *It was possible that there were a few similarities.*

Christian shook his head incredulously. "His hair color, his smile, that weirdly intense look on his face…"

"I don't look weirdly intense before racing," Freddie protested.

"I'm saying that you seem to have a lot in common. Maybe this wasn't such a bad idea. You just can't see it after all those G-forces impacted your brain," Christian teased.

"Seriously, Christian. My life has changed so much. When was the last time we hung out?"

Christian shrugged. "You've got a new set of responsibilities. I understand."

"What did you do last weekend?" Freddie persisted.

Christian thought. "Capri. It was amazing. We would have invited you…"

"You know what I was doing?" Freddie interrupted. "Talking with that lawyer. Trying to sort out the mess that my life has become. I mean, Nicholas is a cool kid and all..."

"A great kid," Christian agreed.

"...but I didn't think it would last this long," Freddie griped. "I haven't been on a date in months, because who is supposed to watch him? I thought he would hate living with me and would be given an alternate arrangement. Now, he's talking about staying."

Freddie rubbed his temples with his hand and returned his eyes to the track. He couldn't spot Nicholas. *Great. Had the kid oversteered? Was he bringing the kart home in a bin?* Suddenly, Freddie heard the familiar sound. *Zoom.* Nicholas whizzed past him, having already completed a lap. Freddie and Christian were stunned. *The kid was a natural!* His turns could be smoother, but Nicholas braked at the right times, accelerated quickly, and was outracing the competition with finesse. Christian hooted and hollered as Nicholas made his second lap.

"Excuse me, Mr. Ridgeport? Are you Nicholas' father?" asked an employee, donning a headset and nametag.

"I'm his guardian."

"He just completed the fastest lap we've had here in years. I noticed this was his first time here. Where have you been training him?"

Nicholas screamed in delight as he made his third lap.

"This is his first time in a kart," Freddie boasted.

"And the kid is already better than his old man," Christian quipped.

"Please bring him again. Nicholas would make a great addition to our Junior League. I've a feeling he'll be a Hot Shoe!" The man slipped two business cards into Freddie's fist. "I'm a big fan of both of yours."

Freddie could have burst with pride. "Thank you. I will." Freddie ran to Nicholas as he pulled to a stop.

Nicholas removed his helmet, revealing an ear-to-ear smile. Freddie embraced Nicholas, and was relieved to feel Nicholas hugging him back.

"Did you see me? Were you watching? That was the most fun I've ever had in my life!" Nicholas shook with excitement. Christian emerged from behind Freddie to add his own praise, and Freddie headed to the MonacoGo office to inquire about the Junior League.

Nicholas was a whiz on the grid, but Freddie would have been proud regardless. Racing for the first time took guts. For the first time since Nicholas had moved in, Freddie felt a shred of hope. Maybe he and Nicholas could work something out after all. One lap at a time.

SIX
Charlotte

"C*lient confidentiality." What a concept!* Charlotte was exhausted from her conversation with the stubborn lawyer. To her surprise, the phone number that her mémé had written down all those years ago was still the right one. She had gotten hold of the receptionist and had pleaded to let them speak with Philip Banks. She had expected more of a fight, but the receptionist had patched her through right away. The conversation with Philip went a little less smoothly. Before she had even had a chance to identify herself, she had blurted out the question that was building inside of her: *who had custody of the Stefano child? Was he safe?* Philip had politely cut her off and informed her about the nature of client confidentiality and that their conversation would go no further.

She hung up and fatigue struck her like a rogue tidal wave. After napping for hours, Charlotte was surprised that she hadn't awoken in a cold sweat, as she usually did back in New York. When she rose, she momentarily wondered where she was, ensconced in crisp white sheets that were not her own. The onslaught of earlier events sank her deeper into the tailormade pillow. Thoughts of a shattered child stampeded through her mind as she peeled her weary body from the mattress.

The Monaco sun reflected from the twinkling Mediterranean, and Charlotte shielded her squinted eyes. From the kitchen, she could hear

Marguerite humming Vivaldi. She always bore hardship beautifully. Her mémé was hobbling around in the kitchen with her cane, insisting on making Charlotte more coffee. She would have protested if she hadn't known the grandmother's wilfulness. Besides, there was nothing worse than treating someone like they were seconds from death.

"*Merci*," Charlotte said as she made her way to the table, gratefully accepting her grandmother's Le Creuset mug filled to the brim with Saint Helena. It tasted just as she remembered.

"We did not hear what we wanted to hear, but we can't focus on that all day. What are you going to do this evening, aside from keeping an old woman company?" Marguerite winked as she sipped her own equally well-poured Molokai mule.

Charlotte recalled that Marguerite typically responded to stress by making plans. Her stoic mémé was always working towards a goal. Even in her grandmother's retirement, there was never a day that passed where she didn't have something she was working towards.

"What are you working on now?" Charlotte asked her mémé. "Any projects on the go?"

Marguerite waved her off. "Nothing important. Now, what are you going to do today?"

Charlotte took a big gulp before answering. "I'm going to help you around the house, mémé," she said with resolve. "That is why I came back, after all."

Her grandmother swatted the air. "Nonsense. I'm already dressed. And the cleaners are coming in an hour. There's nothing for you to do around here. I'm simply delighted to have you back home. Enjoy yourself; that is your *only* goal today."

It had been a long time since Charlotte had a single goal for one day, let alone a goal as lofty as enjoyment. Just the day before, she had a million things to do back in New York City. And that was before getting on the plane to head to Monaco. Charlotte couldn't help but wonder if she was actually doing the helping for her mémé, or if it was the other way around. Either way, Charlotte wasn't going to argue with her grandmother.

"And what do you recommend instead?"

"Why don't you pick up fresh baguette, some lemons, and provolone from the market?"

Charlotte was grateful for the task. "Right away."

Her mémé laughed. "Look at you—such a New Yorker now. In such a hurry." Her grandmother cast a glance at the clock fixed on the wall. "But then again, the market does tend to get busy and the best baguette sells fast. You've had plenty of time to relax by now, *non*?""

As she strolled across Saint-Charles, Charlotte couldn't help focusing on every young boy in her path. *The Stefanos were structured, privileged, and experienced. At their age, they must have arranged a thorough contingency plan for their son.*

The terracotta-colored brick sidewalk injected a bounce into Charlotte's step, and the frequent revving of luxury engines awakened her. The storefronts, each more beautiful than the next, battled for her attention. Corinthian columns and swirling wrought iron decorated the exteriors, and stained glass colored the windows.

I should relax, Charlotte told herself. Nobody in Monaco knew that she had returned. Her photos were taken on her ancient camera and developed. She stayed off of social media, and email was her sole mode of electronic communication. Even then, the only person who she spoke with regularly on the phone was her mémé. It wasn't that Charlotte disliked social media or avoided friendships. Far from it. But privacy was more important to her than anything else. The boundary between her present and past would remain intact.

As Charlotte strolled down the impeccable cobbled sidewalk, she admired the cohesiveness of the manicured park on one side and ivory stucco buildings on the other. *Snap.* She poised her camera towards the sky and captured the sun painting the cascading bougainvillea. As she snapped a perfect shot of the Saint-Charles Church's Neo-Renaissance architecture, the bell tower contrasted against the bright blue sky and preened greenery surrounding it.

Strange, Charlotte thought as she squinted through the lens. A figure in the background looked vaguely recognizable.

"Charlotte?" the familiar voice called to her. The hair upon Charlotte's neck rose and goosebumps pricked her arms. Her body stiffened yet she continued on her way. *Surely, she was hallucinating.*

"Charlotte?" the voice persisted.

She couldn't ignore it. The figure now stood directly before her—the entire six feet and two inches. There was no mistaking him. It was Freddie Ridgeport.

Snap. Her finger triggered the camera in surprise, immortalizing the moment.

He was more handsome than she remembered. Charlotte's heart sank into her stomach as she struggled to tear her gaze from him. Her breaths presented in short shallow bursts and her mind fogged. Time slowed around her, while her breathing continued to quicken. Freddie's skin alluded to a springtime under the Monaco sun, and his retirement was evident in his slackened jaw. She took him in—all of him. This was the moment Charlotte had silently rehearsed for ten years: she would apologize, clarify, and account for the pain she caused. Despite her preparation, her mind was blank and her mouth dry. A lengthy speech was the furthest thing from Charlotte's mind.

Freddie appeared as shocked as Charlotte felt. He froze in her presence, his chest rising and falling ever so slightly after running to catch her. They could have stared in rigid silence for ages. A young boy, trailing after Freddie, broke the silence.

"Freddie, who is that?"

Charlotte broke from Freddie's gaze and gaped at the child, who was eying her with interest. She did a double take. *Freddie had a kid?* Charlotte swallowed shakily. The boy undoubtedly bore similarities.

Finally, Freddie cleared his throat. His eyes crinkled at the corners as he broke a smile. "Hi Charlotte." His slow, soft cadence melted her. "It's good to see you."

Butterflies erupted in Charlotte's stomach. *It was certainly good to see him too.*

"Charlotte?" the little boy echoed.

Freddie jolted to the present and inhaled deeply. "Right. Nicholas, this is Charlotte. Charlotte, this is Nicholas."

Freddie had a son. Charlotte couldn't believe it. Nicholas looked just like him. She smiled, happy that Freddie was living a beautiful life. She glanced at his left hand. *No ring.* Charlotte felt embarrassed for even looking, and even more so at the trill of delight running through her.

Nicholas, a precocious boy, extended his hand to Charlotte. "Pleased to meet you, Charlotte. My name is Nicholas," he announced formally. "I'm the next Formula One superstar."

The nervousness brewing in Charlotte dissipated as she burst into laughter. Wiping her eyes, she looked up to see Freddie doing the same. The little boy, Nicholas, was looking at them both in delighted excitement.

"I'm sure you are," Charlotte said. "You've got a great dad at your fingertips to teach you."

Freddie's jovial expression sobered. "Oh, I'm not his—"

"—He's not my dad," Nicholas jumped in. The boy's expression momentarily saddened before turning hopeful. "But he's my guardian?"

Freddie nodded, appearing vaguely overwhelmed. "That's right. I'm your guardian," he agreed in a tone that Charlotte could not interpret. "I'm his guardian," he repeated. This time, he sounded to be convincing himself.

Why did the two of them keep repeating the word "guardian?" Was Freddie adopting him? Where were his parents? Freddie watched the boy with such tenderness that Charlotte's heart ached. As Freddie stared at Nicholas, Charlotte was free to stare at Freddie. She felt just as she had when she first met him. The flushed cheeks, lightheadedness, and weakness in her knees could not be blamed on shock.

"We just got back from the karting track," Nicholas declared. "Did you know that I might be a prodigy? I am the record holder for the fastest lap at the track. Have you been to MonacoGo, Charlotte? You'd love it."

"No one said *prodigy*," Freddie muttered, rolling his eyes apologetically.

Charlotte beamed. She liked this child. *Who wouldn't?* "Do you race often?" she asked.

"This was my first time," Nicholas explained. "Freddie took me. My parents never took me racing. They were scared that it was too dangerous."

The past tense Nicholas used wasn't lost on Charlotte, and she met Freddie's eyes for confirmation. His saddened expression confirmed her belief: *The boy's parents were dead.* She knew the feeling. Such a shame—Nicholas was so young.

"Cool camera," Nicholas continued, eyeing the vintage piece that hung from her neck. "Can I try it?"

"Of course!" Charlotte eagerly pulled the precious possession over her head. "Press here." She rarely let anybody touch her camera. It was the one of few remaining pieces of her own father—but the child enchanted Charlotte.

"Smile," Nicholas said, snapping a picture of her.

She obeyed, slightly self-conscious.

Nicholas motioned for Freddie to move in. "Now, you put your arm around her," Nicholas ordered.

"No need to be so bossy," Freddie said lightly.

"I don't mind," Charlotte said.

"Well," Freddie shrugged and laughed lightly. "If he insists."

As Freddie wrapped his arm around her, Charlotte fixed her gaze upon Nicholas and the camera, but she couldn't ignore the electric current splicing through her bare shoulders.

Keep it together, Charlotte told herself. Her body rebelled by pressing into Freddie's.

"Nicholas, can you grab some brioche for breakfast tomorrow?" Freddie handed Nicholas a yellow banknote and pointed in the direction of a nearby patisserie. "And don't forget the camera."

"Okay. It was very nice to meet you, Charlotte. And thanks for letting me take those pictures."

Charlotte said goodbye to Nicholas and, as he walked away, her stare remained tethered to his tiny silhouette. She whipped her head back towards Freddie. "He's wonderful."

Freddie shook his head in amusement while Charlotte prayed for the strength to return to her weakened knees. How was it that, after ten years apart, she still felt exactly as she had at eighteen? Charlotte pondered how she might appropriately word her overwhelming questions about Nicholas. Like old times, Freddie understood Charlotte's silence.

"He's the Stefanos' son," Freddie spoke at a hushed volume.

Freddie continued to speak, but Charlotte had stopped listening. Explosions were going off in her head, her neurons and synapses firing on all cylinders. It was like a domino effect, one thought triggering the next, until the pieces were all laid out in a row. Just like her mémé had mentioned the day before, the Stefanos had died tragically in a car accident a few months earlier. She had spent the entire night wondering where their son had gone.

Now she knew.

Her knees now felt weak for all the wrong reasons. Her head was spinning and her heart pounded through her chest. She needed to sit down. She needed a glass of water. Her entire world slowing down, the edges of her vision going into soft-focus.

Nicholas was her biological son. She was Nicholas' biological mother. *Did Freddie have any clue?*

Freddie had stopped talking, matching her silence. "Are you okay?" he asked tentatively.

"I'm fine!" Charlotte said a little too quickly, her throat feeling tight and constricting. She crossed and then uncrossed her arms. "I'm just fine," she said again in what she hoped was a more normal tone.

"I asked if you want to get dinner and you didn't respond. I just want to check that I haven't grown a third eye." Freddie joked. Charlotte pretended to laugh. "It's been ages since I've seen you. Nine years?"

"Ten," Charlotte responded without thought.

Freddie absentmindedly ran his fingers through his hair. "Wow," he exhaled. "Ten years. I'd love to find out what brought you back to Monaco in the first place. Dinner?"

Say "no," Charlotte thought. She needed distance, but couldn't help herself. "I'm looking forward to it," she stammered. The situation unfolded as if Charlotte were observing from above, or viewing a film starring herself.

"Great. Where are you staying?"

"Le Soleil."

"I'll pick you up at eight?"

"Okay," Charlotte managed. She wiped perspiration from her lip. She needed Freddie to leave so she could plant her behind on the cobblestone and allow herself to crumble.

Freddie kissed both of Charlotte's cheeks as he wished her farewell. He smelled of suntan lotion and Acqua Di Parma aftershave. "You look even more beautiful than I remember."

Charlotte returned a feeble smile. "Lovely to see you, Freddie." Even in the most fragile of situations, her politeness remained intact. She watched agonizingly from a distance as Freddie helped Nicholas handle two large brown paper bags, almost the size of Nicholas' torso. She wanted to chase after them, but her feet constrained her to the bumpy sidewalk. Long after the two had gone, Charlotte stood, planted, replaying the incident in her mind.

As a child, Charlotte would swim as far into the depths of the Mediterranean as she could, causing her to return to the surface gasping for air. This felt just like that.

With a history spanning over a decade, Charlotte and Freddie had attended high school together and like her, Freddie had seemed to be an outsider. He had spent his lunches at this racetrack.
There were rumors that he was training as a racecar driver with teams interested in him.
Charlotte hadn't known much about that world, but she knew that he left school every day on time—presumably to go to the track.

Although Monaco was sunny three hundred days of the year, there was the odd downpour that came quickly and without much warning. She and Freddie had left the school at the same time. She remembered feeling his eyes on her, which had sent a tingle down her spine. Before she made a bolt for it through the rain, Freddie had offered her a drive home from school in his car. She had declined, since she didn't know him after all, but couldn't help feel a tug in her heart towards him. There was something about his lopsided grin, his calm eyes, and that nearly jet-black hair that he slicked back. Like her, he hadn't seemed to have a lot of friends to fall back on—she had recently transferred to that school in Monaco and Freddie was quiet and seemed to spend all of his time racing. That wasn't to say that people at the school didn't have crushes on him—they certainly did. But Freddie had never seemed to take notice of anyone else at the school before her. Something about him and the way he looked at her made her want to tell him all about herself. She had fought that urge as long as she could.

After that day, nothing was the same. Freddie would see her in the hallways and his face would light up. The two of them would talk for as long as the bell would allow. She would blush furiously, always trying to hide it. It was no use—Charlotte had a full-blown crush the moment Freddie had offered her that ride. The following week was sunny and it was the second time he offered to drive her home. It would have been an easy walk back to Le Soleil. Charlotte had smiled and happily accepted the offer.

Even as an adult, she couldn't ignore the fact that Freddie had gotten her through what easily could have been a catastrophic phase of her life. From age sixteen onwards, Freddie had become her first real friend and later her first real—and *only*—love. Their worlds had collided exactly at the right moment when they had needed each other the most. The two of them faced similar wars internally—their circumstances unique enough to need the other and similar enough to understand. Their strengths complimented one another. They had fallen for each other fast. After that first drive home, the two of them had laughed about their teachers, how weird and wonderful Monaco was (both of them being transplants) and their mutual excitement to graduate. Freddie had invited her to the track. He had told her that he didn't have too much free time with school and racing, and that the only place he really felt like himself was there. Would she like to come?

Yes, a thousand times.

Before long, it was Charlotte's sanctuary too. She studied on the sidelines, absorbing Freddie's vigor and channeling it into her schoolwork. And when Freddie credited her for his progress, Charlotte felt that she, herself, had won the race.

Freddie would always drive her home afterwards. He kissed her after the first week of her coming to the track and with all the butterflies that fluttered in her stomach, Charlotte felt like she had won a Grand Prix herself.

The two of them became inseparable. In the hallway, those initial shy smiles were now replaced by running up to him and wrapping her arms around his neck and her legs around his waist. They were like magnets. After he finished at the track after school, those car rides where he drove her back home became longer and longer. On those drives, they slowly shared their stories to each other. Little by little, their secrets came out.

On a winding drive as the sun was going down, Charlotte told Freddie the story of her family—how her mother had ended her own life, her father had died in an accident a year later, and the whole story that came before that. The words that escaped her lips didn't sound like hers. She had never talked about any of that before to anyone. In the Levant household, ugliness was not discussed. It was swept under rugs, vacuumed away, and certainly never to be brought out and examined with another person.

Freddie had said nothing. He listened quietly, offering sad smiles and hand squeezes when appropriate. Simply talking was the easiest and hardest thing in the world. At the time the words had spilled out of her, but sharing that again felt impossible.

Although it took him a little longer to open up, Freddie spoke about his own life and how his experience led him to where he is now. In some ways, he said he felt grateful for the difficult upbringing he had. He would never have become the racer he was now—with the ambition, passion, and desire to do it all the time—if life at home had been all roses.

Those early, vulnerable disclosures were important foundational moments. Talking was both the easiest and hardest act. The couple often discussed life after graduation. Freddie knew exactly what he was going to do. His racing became obsessive and competitive. Charlotte would have done anything to aid his dream of being a Formula One driver. As for her own future, Charlotte had never been quite sure, always idealizing new plans that appealed to her more than those from the day before.

Freddie Ridgeport was undeniably the love of Charlotte's life. She knew it then and now. Freddie was her daredevil with a golden heart. He had gifted her stability, certainty, and comfort that no person—not even her beloved mémé—had ever provided.

When her pregnancy test was positive, Charlotte panicked. *A baby could impede Freddie's dreams,* she thought.

Freddie's father validated her concern. One evening, after dinner at the Ridgeports', Stewart Ridgeport caught Charlotte alone. "You care about Freddie, isn't that right? The Number One goal is for him to succeed. And little Freddies running around would ruin his focus, his hard work, his plans, and his future. All down the drain. You can't become the best at anything, let alone get a seat on a team, if you're providing for a family. He can't commit to anything other than winning right now—not you and certainly not any little versions of the two of you running around. You understand?"

Charlotte could still hear Stewart's voice in her head with crystal clarity. After his speech, Charlotte complied. Her queasiness doubled. *How had he known?*

Freddie joined a professional racing team in an entry-level position, and Charlotte couldn't stop weeping. As Freddie continued texting her about his escalating success, she became avoidant. The pressure of a balloon nearing its bursting point built inside of her. Though reluctant, Charlotte had to tell Marguerite, who could hear Charlotte's sobs through the glossy bedroom door. *Surely, her mémé would know what to do.*

As Charlotte isolated herself, Freddie relentlessly tried to reach her. Charlotte and Marguerite hid from the repetitive sounds of the brass knocker and telephone. The balcony doors and curtains remained closed. Freddie waited in the Le Soleil lobby for hours, hoping to catch Charlotte or Marguerite as they passed through. Marguerite eventually told Freddie that Charlotte had a stomach flu, which wasn't entirely untrue, for Charlotte was regularly vomiting from nervousness and morning sickness.

Every option was entertained. The world had lost too much of her family already to terminate. Depending on Freddie and his parents was out of the question. A teenager and her grandmother made a less than ideal team for raising a newborn. Adoption seemed like the only sensible choice.

Marguerite promised that the baby would be adopted by a loving family, and given the best possible life. She took Charlotte to a town in Northern France, where her anonymity was protected, and arranged an adoption with her cherished friends, Isabelle and Roland Stefano. Charlotte agreed to meet with the Stefanos on the condition of complete and total secrecy. She had met the older couple before on numerous occasions but this time, it was completely different. Marguerite had her dear friends sign a legal waiver, ensuring their secrecy about Charlotte's pregnancy no matter what transpired. The father of the child was never discussed, although both the Stefanos knew that Charlotte had been dating Freddie. Unable to conceive during their youth, the still-vivacious Stefanos yearned for a child. Upon her approval, she signed the document drawn up by their lawyer, which finalized the Stefanos' legal adoption of her child after their birth.

By that point, Charlotte had disappeared from Freddie's life, which broke her heart. She tried to justify it. *Relationships always ended in heartache, anyway. Freddie's father was right. She was saving him.* Charlotte was taking herself out of the equation, allowing Freddie to be truly happy. Without any distractions, he would be able to succeed in his mission in life. She was only going to get in the way, and a baby certainly couldn't factor into that. Freddie's father perhaps was right, although Charlotte hated to admit it.

In that Northern town in France, along the border of France and Belgium, she stayed in an apartment her mémé had rented for her and spent that summer gorging on croissants, baguette, cheeses, and olives. Olives were a craving that became nearly insatiable. Her stomach grew and sometimes she felt a kick, which she steadfastly ignored. Marguerite set her up with a doctor, who she met for check-ups every few weeks. Whenever Charlotte began to doubt her decision, she would immediately distract herself by going for a walk or watching TV—anything to keep her from thinking about the present moment and what her life had become.

When the time came to give birth, Charlotte was in a trance.

She knew that she couldn't be a parent. Charlotte wept as she held that perfect baby in her arms, her heart swelling and breaking simultaneously. Being the mother that the child deserved would have been impossible. She was raised by an emotionally absent mother who eventually took her own life. Her father, as hard as he tried, hadn't been around much before he died. Eighteen year-old Charlotte was still dealing with their deaths.

Charlotte planned to part with the baby immediately after his birth, but she held him. It was the happiest and saddest hour. His round eyes matched the color of the sea beside which he was created. She whispered promises into his tiny ears, assuring him and herself that she was doing the right thing. She promised a family that loved, and was ready, for him.

Promises were strange, though. *Who were they made for?* Charlotte was desperate for certainty when the nurse arrived to take the boy to his adoptive parents. Her heart sank into her stomach. With one final indelible look into her baby's eyes, she said "goodbye" for what she believed to be the last time.

Charlotte wouldn't have guessed that, ten years later, she would be saying "goodbye" to that angel once more, and watching him depart on his own two feet. As the child—*her* child—waltzed down that winding street in Monaco with Freddie by his side, her heart swelled and ruptured, just like it had before. *All of those feelings for Freddie. All of that love for Nicholas.* It hadn't disappeared. It had merely hid from plain sight for a little while.

Keep it light and keep it shiny.

Though nobody was watching, Charlotte forced a smile as tears threatened to slip from her eyes. Why did she put so much pressure on herself to be okay? She had been asked that question before, by someone she had dated (and consequently dumped). The mistake she made—the really big mistake she made—was too unruly to tidy up.

Charlotte had been certain of her secret's security, because the few people who knew of it had a similarly vested interest in its protection. With the Stefanos gone, she wasn't sure how to keep the truth from rising. When she painstakingly let go of her son, Charlotte imagined his privileged future in the happiest of homes, where he would grow into a beautiful, ambitious, talented, and well-adjusted soul. *This* wasn't what she had wanted. *This* wasn't what Nicholas deserved.

Charlotte felt doubt stirring. Threatening and unyielding, Charlotte pushed it deep inside of her, as she always had. With the Stefanos gone, she was no longer confident in her ability to contain this secret. *How would Nicholas and Freddie feel? The truth could ruin lives.* Charlotte would do whatever it took to conceal that truth, regardless of the cost.

SEVEN

Freddie

A decade-long list of questions for Charlotte consumed Freddie's mind. But when he saw her, all he wanted to know was how she was.

Freddie couldn't believe his luck. He was in pole position for a second chance. His world was a series of surprises, especially within the last few months. *Charlotte Levant, in the flesh, right here in Monaco.*

Freddie looked down at the kid. *The kid! Who would watch him during Freddie's date?* He mulled over potential contacts as he neared the Port Hercule, but could envision only Charlotte. Freddie refused to leave Nicholas in the care of a stranger or—worse—his friends. *Was Nicholas old enough to stay home alone?* Freddie gazed down at Nicholas as they passed the ornate wrought iron lampposts. Nicholas audibly sniffed the electric pink bougainvillea, which spilled off of buildings.

"They smell like summer," Nicholas declared.

"Have you ever stayed at home by yourself?" Freddie asked tentatively.

Nicholas' eyes widened. "No, but I've always wanted to. Oh please? Please?"

Momentarily relieved, Freddie laughed in delight. "Yes. Great."

"I'm going to have a huge party," Nicholas insisted with wistful hope. "We'll make pizza and pasta, and everyone will have the best time!"

Freddie sighed. *Never mind.* He would have to figure out something else.

"Look over there!" The kid pointed at tourists photographing Freddie from underneath their straw fedoras.

It didn't matter. Charlotte had returned, the sun was shining, and Freddie finally made progress with Nicholas. He graced the fawning group with a brief smile and wave.

"Smile," he instructed Nicholas, nudging him and laughing, but Nicholas was already snapping his own photos of Freddie's murmuring admirers.

Freddie pulled Nicholas down a narrow walkway, peppered with small restaurants and colorful window boxes.

"One day, they'll want pictures of me," Nicholas declared.

Freddie laughed again, noticing the confidence that the Stefanos had instilled in Nicholas. Freddie, who rarely thought of his own childhood, found himself wishing that he'd been given such a gift when he was a boy.

Freddie's model for 'good' parenting wasn't inspired by his upbringing. Freddie had grown up in an economically wealthy, but emotionally impoverished, household. His unspeakably competitive and ruthless father, Stewart Ridgeport, hadn't believed that Freddie could achieve tremendous success, especially as a racecar driver. Freddie's determination to prove his father wrong pushed him to unprecedented heights—or, in his case, *speeds.* His father's immense shock made Freddie's success even sweeter.

With a mother addicted to the bottle and no siblings, Freddie was Stewart's sole target. Stewart regularly berated Freddie's failures and perceived shortcomings. Stewart noticed when Freddie scored a B on a test, or didn't have a girlfriend or enough friends. After years of verbal abuse, Freddie found solace in go-karting.

Freddie's foray into racing was an accident, after a friend suggested it offhandedly. Freddie hadn't been exposed to racing before then, aside from marveling at his father's collection of exotic cars.

Racing wiped away any rumination of his father's words. *It was just him and the car.*

To make 'home' a safe place for Nicholas, Freddie had to throw his father's practices into reverse. "I'm sure that after years of training, people will want pictures with you, Nicholas. But just remember," he paused dramatically, hoping to convince the kid that he was imparting fatherly wisdom. "Nothing feels as good as winning."

Nicholas nodded studiously. "I reckon I'll get there in a year."

Freddie laughed. "I'm sure you will, kid. I'm sure you will."

The two of them lapsed into silence as they walked along Port Hercules.

"Who are you texting?" Freddie asked, realizing that he knew little about the kid's phone use.

"I'm not texting," Nicholas replied. "I'm looking at the racing stats this year."

Freddie nodded, impressed by Nicholas' discipline. "You're serious about this, aren't you?"

Nicholas looked up at Freddie. "Yes, sir."

Things were finally happening as they were supposed to. Nicholas had led Freddie back to Charlotte. As always, racing was his *in.* He had never fallen in love with anyone else. For so many, time allows love to fade, but the opposite was true for Freddie. His love for Charlotte had simmered, gained force, and evolved into a wildfire.

Freddie gathered that Nicholas was no social butterfly. Before and after school, the kid always waited alone. Nicholas had insisted that he had friends, but Freddie worried. He resisted the urge to prod, though, remembering his own father's obsession with his social status.

Freddie still didn't know what to do with Nicholas that evening. He *had* to see Charlotte. Rescheduling was out of the question. *Would bringing Nicholas along ruin everything? Was it possible that it could even be...endearing?*

"I'm thinking about when we're going to go racing again," Nicholas said. "When do you think we will go again, Freddie?"

Witnessing a nine year-old find his strength and resiliency was a new experience for Freddie. "Whenever you like."

"How about this evening?" Nicholas pressed.

Freddie squatted beside the kid. He needed a solution. "We can go racing again tonight at MonacoGo. But only if Charlotte comes with us."

Nicholas' grin widened, and he enveloped Freddie in a hug for the first time. Freddie was shocked, and unexpectedly emotional. *What was that feeling?* He had never felt it before.

Running into Charlotte hadn't been the intimate rendezvous Freddie would have planned. In a perfect world, Freddie would meet Charlotte for a sunset stroll along the same path he and Nicholas walked, adjacent to Port Hercule. Freddie would be alone, and Charlotte would suggest a drink at the nearest bar. Of course, if everything in his life ran smoothly, Charlotte would have never left in the first place.

That night, he would pick her up at Le Soleil and explain Nicholas' attendance, and the three of them would head to the karting track. Hopefully, Charlotte was still as easygoing as Freddie remembered. Perhaps, they could squeeze in a more glamorous dinner after Nicholas fell asleep, but specific plans didn't matter to Freddie. The only plan that mattered was winning Charlotte back, *no matter what.*

Regardless of what had happened, she had said "yes" to meeting him again! And Nicholas had been so charming. Immediately, he had panicked thinking she must have assumed he was married or in a relationship with a son. Sending Nicholas to that patisserie turned out to be a lifesaver. It was a small chance to tell her the truth. Although he had done his best to explain the situation to her as well as he could, given how out-of-sorts he had felt, he wasn't sure that the message translated loud and clear: Nicholas wasn't his son. Nicholas was the child of which he was the legal guardian, by some strange twist of fate. Surely she would have questions.

His heart thudded in his chest. Had he even bothered to check her left hand? Could Charlotte be married?

He felt sick at the thought of finally reuniting with Charlotte, only to potentially realize that she did not consider their dinner a 'date' as he did, and simply a dinner. Could there be anything more embarrassing?

"Hey, Nicholas, do you have Instagram?"

Nicholas laughed. "Yes. Everyone does."

Freddie had downloaded the app onto his phone, took one picture of himself at the Grand Prix, swiftly forgot his password, and that was the end of it.

"Can you look up Charlotte Levant?"

Nicholas began to punch at the phone with both hands, frowning. "There's nothing…" he said in a bored tone, as he swiped his finger down the screen. "Maybe she goes by a different name."

If Charlotte had married and taken another person's last name, that would explain things. But Freddie had tried finding Charlotte on social media before. Years earlier, he had even tried reaching out to her grandmother, Marguerite Levant, but she had told him politely that she wasn't at liberty to disclose Charlotte's private information. He had wished that he were less of a gentleman. Perhaps if he hadn't said that he understood, maybe he would have gotten more information. But there could have been the chance that Marguerite would have told the rest of Monaco he was a lunatic, still in love with a ghost.

Marguerite Levant was a kind woman. He thought highly of her. But he also thought that some of Charlotte's trauma from her childhood must have surfaced before she left, creating a situation where she felt the need to escape Monaco entirely. Freddie couldn't blame her. At times, he had wanted to do the exact same thing. He had run into Marguerite at the farmer's market and at restaurants over the years. At first, Freddie had panicked and asked her about Charlotte. Marguerite's feathers never seemed to ruffle. She had also looked at him with sympathy and told him that she couldn't tell him anything more, but that Charlotte was okay.

How long had he waited for Charlotte to return to Monaco? With crystal clarity, Freddie could remember the last time he had seen her. If he had known then that it was the last time he would see

Charlotte for ten years, he would have done things totally differently. She had come over to his parents' apartment in Monaco, where the two of them had watched movies and eaten popcorn. They had fooled around underneath the blanket. At the time, he had been thinking of proposing in the near future. Although they were young, Freddie was certain that Charlotte was his wife. He just hadn't popped the question yet.

He had grand plans back then and the future seemed endlessly rosy. His dad's contract was nearing an end and although Steward and Janice Ridgeport were looking forward to their return to Kentucky, he was planning to stay in Monaco. Stewart was hard on him and demanded success. Even though his parents supported his dream to drive in F1 from a financial standpoint (karting and private lessons were an endless expense), they would have preferred if he had followed in Stewart's footsteps and gone in business. If it meant working with his father, Freddie couldn't think of anything worse. No, he would remain in Monaco, continue to train, and eventually work his way up to become a racecar driver. Charlotte would come with him to all his races and he would eventually propose.

But everything had changed overnight.

Charlotte stopped returning his phone calls. She didn't show up to their final few classes of the semester. She never showed up to their pre-scheduled plans to go on a beach walk and he had been left at sunset all on his own. When he had gone to Le Soleil to see what had happened, the concierge hadn't let him up. Immediately, his mind had flitted to the worse case scenarios before he forced himself to focus. Charlotte wasn't dead—*probably*. This was confirmed by Charlotte's grandmother, who had agreed to speak with him as he used the concierge phone. Always affable and warm, Marguerite sounded nothing like herself as she said with steely resolve that Charlotte wasn't going to be in school anymore. She was feeling unwell and couldn't speak with him. His heart had sunk and he had no clue that the worst was yet to come. When Marguerite told him that he wouldn't be able to see Charlotte anymore, he found himself fighting back tears. As he protested, his voice escalating and pleading to let him at least speak with her, the phone line went dead.

Freddie couldn't understand it. He wracked his brain for anything that could have set this off. It didn't make sense. There were no clues she had given him that things weren't going well—not one. In fact, she had told him that she loved him on that last day of theirs together. The only thing that made Freddie feel slightly uneasy about their last day together was when he came back to the living room from the kitchen with a second large bowl of popcorn, recalling his father was speaking to Charlotte. His father practically never left his study while at home. But he hadn't thought much of it. When he had asked Charlotte what they had discussed, she had brushed it off and told him it was nothing. He was so stupid to have believed her, he thought. Freddie confronted his father later that week after he arrived home from a long day of work. Stewart had sighed as if he hadn't the time for trivial conversations, threw his briefcase on the sofa, and spoke plainly. It shattered Freddie's heart to hear his father say that he had told Charlotte that she would be a distraction to him. That's all the information Stewart would give away, and as Freddie screamed at his father for the first time in his life, his father laughed it off and shut his office door. He had never felt so enraged and that night he couldn't sleep.

Just like in his racing practice, Freddie didn't give up. He showed up every day to the lobby of Le Soleil certain that today would be the day Charlotte spoke to him. He needed her to know that his father was wrong; she wouldn't be a distraction to his racing career. But as his attempts were thwarted with zero acknowledgements, the time he spent waiting in that lobby eventually did cut into his racing time. Freddie started spending more time on the grid. When he raced, everything in his mind would empty. It was just him and the car and the track. That outlet and distraction became his savior. Before long, he was winning races consistently. A lot of the other drivers had fathers, uncles, or relatives as their coaches—people invested in their future with every fiber of their soul. Not Freddie. He had stopped talking to his father after that night, not that his father had made any attempt to communicate with him either. He had a hired coach, Mario Vessani, who he had gotten closer with during that time. Mario was pleased with the time, devotion, and focus that Freddie put into his driving that year. Freddie's hunger for success grew and his focus narrowed. It was the perfect storm for success—youth, ambition, and dash of suffering. Freddie knew he had what it took to succeed. Mario knew he had what it took to succeed.

Charlotte vanishing was the dose of motivation he had needed—perhaps if he became an F1 driver and started winning Grand Prix's and podiums, then she would come back to him. Then she would realize that his father was wrong, and even if he had been right, it wouldn't matter anymore because she wouldn't be a distraction. He would have already garnered the fame and success that he wanted for himself, that his father knew he was capable of, and that Charlotte believed would make him happy.

"Do you think that Charlotte likes racing?" Nicholas asked, torqueing Freddie away from his thoughts and back to the present.

"Oh, unquestionably," Freddie replied without hesitation.

"I can't wait to race Charlotte. Will you race with us too?"

"Uh, let's see how the evening goes," Freddie said. His plan for now was to let Nicholas race and it would give him and Charlotte the privacy they needed from the sidelines.

Taking Charlotte on their date was the perfect qualifying lap for their relationship. It was a chance to test the grid and see if there were any sharp turns. More than anything, Freddie hoped that this evening would turbocharge the sparks they had for one another.

"Come on," Freddie said, his mood perking up. "Lets get you a gelato." He had planned to get Nicholas one in case of failure. He wouldn't have anticipated so much success...for *both* of them. He looked down at Nicholas, who was practically bouncing to the gelato shop. Could Nicholas be his good luck charm?

His one hope was that this date would give them the traction they needed to win. And Freddie was used to winning.

EIGHT
Charlotte

Charlotte was almost back at Le Soleil with the items her mémé had requested. Her hands shook as she walked down the street, the sun beating down on her. Everything felt surreal. Seeing Freddie. Seeing him with that kid. Realizing who that kid was! *Nicholas.* He tugged at her heartstrings. *He was beautiful.*

Pride, regret, anger, and love swirled into a distracting cocktail. *How would she navigate that evening?* Still reeling, Charlotte hardly noticed the woman walking towards her.

"Charlotte Levant?"

Charlotte turned to see a woman she didn't recognize, with heavily highlighted hair and even more heavily applied eyeliner. The woman was beautiful—in an overly preened way. Charlotte was hardly in a headspace to chat, but surely this was an old friend. True to herself, Charlotte politely smiled at the stranger, despite wanting nothing more than privacy.

The woman burst into fits of laughter. "You must not recognize me," the stranger stated obnoxiously, tapping on her nose and winking. "I look a bit different now."

Charlotte's brow furrowed. Recalling faces felt impossible after shutting out the past for so long, but, blocking out the visual, Charlotte recognized something about the woman's nasal voice. The familiarity triggered panic, but Charlotte still couldn't identify her.

"Violet. Violet Macintyre," the woman proclaimed. "*Surely*, you must remember me."

Layers of Charlotte's memory peeled back, slowly revealing the remnants of her previous life. Violet was Charlotte's classmate in high school. Although they hadn't been friends, they were definitely not enemies either. A vague recollection of Violet's tendency to talk poorly about her peers struck Charlotte. Even in her youth, Charlotte knew that when people talked badly about others *to* you, they would soon talk badly *about* you—if they weren't already doing so. She kept a friendly distance but harbored no resentment towards Violet. Charlotte hadn't even thought about her since she left Monaco.

Charlotte nodded quickly. "Right, Violet. Wow, it's been quite a while. How are you?"

Violet's eyes lit up predatorily as she slid closer to Charlotte. "Excellent, thanks. Did I see you with Freddie back there?" Her expression was unyieldingly interested, like a lion cornering its prey.

Charlotte took a deep breath. Immediately, she remembered why she needed to leave Monaco—it was too small of a country to hide such a big secret. "I suppose so, yes—"

"—I knew it!" Violet interrupted. Her eyes narrowed. "And that kid? Do you know who on Earth he is?"

Charlotte gulped. *Barely a hello* before Violet accosted her for gossip and private information. *This person hadn't changed.* Some people never did.

"I'm afraid that I don't have much time to catch up today and I have to get going," she managed as she looked at her watch and pulled a face. She'd do anything to evade this line of questioning. "But it was delightful seeing you."

Violet smiled icily. "Yes, just lovely. We should do lunch sometime, if it's not too weird."

"Weird?" Charlotte echoed absently. She bit her lip, realizing she'd fallen into a trap.

"Oh, you know," Violet smiled and twirled a lock of her hair.

"Because of Freddie and my history."

Charlotte tried to maintain composure, but her eyes must have shown her surprise.

Violet narrowed in. "Oh, you didn't know," Violet drawled as she feigned ignorance. "Yes, Freddie and I were an item for quite some time. *Very* serious relationship and all. But I ended things with him. He's still heartbroken. Poor boy. Anyways, it was great to see you. I'm sure I'll see you around and we *must* have lunch."

Violet turned on her heel and walked away with a smirk, leaving a tightening knot inside Charlotte's stomach. *Violet was trying to undercut her.* Charlotte forced herself to wave, just as her mémé had taught her. "Composure under pressure is the ultimate elegance," Marguerite advised. *Anyone could be a hothead. Only few could keep cool amidst flames.* If she had yielded to her emotions, Charlotte would have been screaming, laughing, or both.

Freddie and *Violet?* It seemed like an impossible match. Was it possible that Violet was bluffing? After ten years, Charlotte couldn't know what—or more specifically, *who*—Freddie was into anymore. Charlotte watched from afar as Violet trotted away in her stiletto heels. Anywhere that woman went, Charlotte was certain that chaos followed. Violet was trouble, but from Charlotte's understanding, she was also clueless. For that reason, Charlotte wouldn't have cared if Violet was Freddie's ex-*wife.* Violet clearly knew nothing about Nicholas, or his true relationship to Freddie. With Violet unaware, Charlotte was assured that the rest of Monaco was too.

Charlotte had a million questions. *How were Freddie and Nicholas getting along? Were either of them suspicious? How hadn't anyone else found out? How would she protect Nicholas and Freddie from the truth?* If Violet represented people's curiosity in Monaco, the country would soon be clawing for details about the famous racer and his lovechild. But that was fine, because Charlotte could be fierce too. Once having been described as a lion in sheep's clothing, and not in a bad way, only a few people knew that side to her—Freddie being one of them. He had been the one to call her that. Few people knew the real her. The protective and loyal side to her.

Clutching her items and her camera, Charlotte's eyes narrowed as she walked back home with a newfound determination in her step. Right now, she had business to see to.

She could be shocked and surprised later; she didn't have time for that right now. Right now, she had a duty and a responsibility. It came with her actions. And she certainly didn't want to be in this position, but she knew that she needed to protect Freddie and Nicholas. No one, *certainly* not Violet Macintyre, was going to get in her way. She had worked too hard, suffered too long, and sacrificed too much for the truth to be derailed so easily. Even the whiff of that being a possibility was too dangerous. She needed to squelch any questions about why the Stefanos had chosen Freddie to be Nicholas' guardian… and fast.

But first things first: she would go on a quick dinner with Freddie and Nicholas that evening. It would serve two purposes: Just to ensure that the two of them were getting along well and to find out more information about what Freddie knew. This was a fact-finding mission *only*. No emotions. Clean and simple. Tidy. She would be in and out of their lives before they knew it, getting only the information she needed to make sure she could sleep for the rest of her life.

Perhaps even Nicholas was the one who knew something. She *had* to find out. It simply couldn't be left up to chance. The fact that the dinner may ease the anxious part of her mind, the part of her brain that always wondered how Nicholas was doing, that was just a bonus. Right now, protecting Nicholas came first.

She took a deep breath of salty sea air, feeling as refreshed as she had when she first came to Monaco all of those years earlier. The sun was pouring over her, making the sea shimmer and the convertible tops fold down. The patios were filling up and the sidewalks were steadily filling with tourists, looking eager with their cameras, just like her.

But she wasn't a tourist, even though she was a visitor to that magnificent country just like them. A family smiled at her as they passed by. Charlotte found herself smiling back, even giving a little wave to the children.

She felt her heart skip a beat as she arrived back at Le Soleil. Just a quick dinner, she told herself. But maybe not *too* quick. She needed to do her due diligence to ensure that both he and the child were all right. Then, she would be gone from their lives. One quick little dinner with Freddie. The sun seemed to be radiating from within her rather than from above. A few bites, a bit of conversation, and that would be the end of it. After all, what was the harm in that?

NINE

Violet

Violet Macintyre prayed that her credit card would go through as she ferociously devoured the final bites of her salad. She was livid.

Charlotte Levant, who had tormented her during her entire relationship with Freddie, had the audacity to not even remember who she was? During her relationship, Violet comforted herself with the thought of Charlotte stalking her socials and envying her glow-up. Unless Charlotte was a secretly top-notch actress, which she was certain she wasn't, Charlotte hadn't even recognized her. Violet bitterly recalled Charlotte's basic, modest outfit. Of course someone like Charlotte could throw on something entirely uncreative and still be treated like a queen. Unlike Violet, Charlotte didn't have to be hot. Charlotte didn't have to be flashy.

Violet was barely employed, but still had a full-time job – of fitting in. In Monaco, wealth and status were tough to fake. Violet knew the basics. There was something, though – an aura – about girls like Charlotte. You just knew they were somebody. And the less they tried, the higher they reigned. The same rules didn't apply to Violet. Violet in six-inch pumps, the most sought-after couture, and push-up bra to the stars didn't compare to Charlotte in her white and beige ensemble.

She hadn't meant to be quite so *prying* when she saw Charlotte Levant. Violet was aware that she ambushed people who she perceived as a threat. She was working on it, but she was caught off guard today. That girl, Charlotte, was her worst nightmare when she and Freddie were together. Charlotte had dated him a million years before Violet came into the picture and, still, her name was stuck in Freddie's mouth like a canker sore—or a leech. Violet tried everything short of renaming herself 'Charlotte' to seduce Freddie into obsessing over *her* instead, but Violet was a backmarker, stuck behind Charlotte's dirty air. It got so bad that whenever Freddie heard someone say the name 'Charlotte' in public, he'd pathetically look up from whatever he was doing and scan the area like a lost dog. Violet responded with nonchalant eye-rolls and artificial indifference, but, truthfully, Freddie's lovesick pitifulness grossed her out. Violet felt insecure throughout the entire year that they'd dated, and she shuddered at the thought of Charlotte's physical presence. Today, her fear came true, and she was powerless—Violet wasn't part of Freddie's life anymore.

When she saw Freddie, she desperately wanted to plead for forgiveness, and put his hands on all of the things he surely still liked about her. But then she saw Charlotte. Even from a distance, Violet knew they were picking up from where they had left off. It was obvious by the way he draped his arm around her that they were an item now, and a stab of fury shot through her. *What was so enticing about Charlotte?* Violet couldn't imagine what boring Charlotte offered Freddie that she didn't.

Violet looked down at the shiny diamond on her left ring finger. It had been there for a month, but still felt foreign. She tried not to frown at it, for her Botox had recently worn off, and her credit cards couldn't yet accommodate her next dose. "If you don't fold the paper, it won't crease," the medical technician had dumbly explained. She pressed her left thumb between her microshaded eyebrows. Wasn't this what she always wanted? A glamorous life in Monaco with a fiancé who loved her? Finally, she wouldn't have to worry. She gnawed at the tip of a breadstick, hoping to quell the anxiety. Outperforming the car sure sounded nice, but as she ready for the ride?

Mrs. Violet Blitzgrav. Blitz*grave* more like. Maybe it suited her.

I'm marrying the wrong racer. She took a deep swig of her sparkling wine and begged the annoying voice in her head to shut up. Yanic Blitzgrav may not have been the hottest racing legend on the market, but golddiggers can't be choosers. He wasn't Freddie, but at least Yanic didn't have her endlessly vying for his attention.

Her waiter returned with her credit card and paid bill. Violet wasn't easily embarrassed, but a declined payment would have mortified her. Violet assumed that the people around her were always watching, like she was. She worried about her clueless fiancé, racing legend Yanic Blitzgrav, discovering her financial reality. Sometimes, she worried almost enough to stop her from spending nonexistent money in public.

"*Merci*," Violet winked at the waiter. It was the middle of the afternoon. She had already exercised with her personal trainer, an extravagant gift from her husband-to-be. She had run into Charlotte Levant, and had now had a light lunch to fill the first half of the day. Now what? What was she going to do with the rest of her day? She had already read herself nearly to death and she wasn't a huge fan of anything on T.V. Maybe an Instagram photoshoot?

Violet headed back to her apartment. Soon, she wouldn't have to pay that exorbitant rent. The scam products that she promoted only covered so many expenses. Soon, she would be living with her *lovely* husband and stepson-to-be. "*Lovely.*" A word Charlotte probably used.

Violet's skin crawled when she thought about Yanic's kid, Pierre. Children made her feel *sticky* and *itchy*. Yanic wasn't privy to Violet's aversion—but Freddie was. Violet was still yearning to know who that little boy was.

A text message popped up on her screen.

"*What's the scoop this week?*"

Violet groaned. She typed back quickly, "*It's on the way Randolph, and it's really juicy.*" She was fibbing, of course, but the editor from the online tabloid *La Mode and Monde* didn't know that. It had been a slow month for celebrity and socialite gossip. A slow *few* months. Violet could prove that with her bank account, not that she ever would.

Falling in love with Freddie hadn't been part of Violet's plan. Secretly, she had harbored a small crush on him since high school and, after all those years, she felt butterflies in her stomach when she got the chance to interview him. She mentioned that they had attended high school together, but he hadn't remembered her. Of course, she had remembered him.

Violet knew that men were easily seduced by lengthy conversations about themselves, and keeping Freddie engaged in conversation was especially easy due to their shared interest in racing. However, Violet didn't know that the world was cruel to girls who tried to 'have it all.' Dating Freddie led to her professional termination. "Conflict of interest," she was told. Violet didn't even bother to fight back. She was the romantic partner of one of their most valuable interviewees, which made *her* valuable. She would leave gracefully, but she was taking their prized asset along with her.

Maintaining her intentional haughtiness became tiresome as Violet's confidence succumbed to the loss of her career. She tried leveraging her relationship in exchange for new opportunities, but Freddie was surprisingly uninfluential. Without income, Violet started to exploit her less intellectual assets. As Freddie's arm candy, she appealed to a niche online crowd of try-too-hard teen girls, but her sales were scarce.

Violet disliked children, and she disliked parents even more—especially her own. She resented her unsustainably privileged upbringing, and felt that "riches-to-rags" qualified as a disability. Violet's luxurious childhood in Monaco was cut short after her father abandoned the family. Her adolescence was spent bouncing around Europe with her mother. There was always a new step-father, and always a new address. Even as an adult, Violet couldn't connect to people or places easily. A few years ago, after many "homes," Violet's love of motor racing brought her back to Monaco with a simple and clear goal: to be a racing journalist. Violet acquired a job as a reporter for a small online newspaper, to write about F1 and racing.

More recently, Violet's dreams had taken a sharp turn. She unwittingly betrayed her career by falling in love with her subject. That appeared to be a cardinal sin in her world: don't fall for the person you're interviewing. It ruined her journalistic integrity, even if it was for a small press. She took herself and her work very seriously. She found another means of work to supplement her income and, in doing so, betrayed Freddie. She didn't attach her name to that work though. At least, not publicly.

Monaco was *quite* an expensive place to live. She had planned to sell one, maybe two of Freddie's personal stories to Randolph. She had made the connection with Randolph from her former experience as a journalist and although she had never thought highly of the magazine or Randolph, it was easy money and she needed it. Fast. Her rent was due and she had felt too prideful to ever ask Freddie for money. She had sold the most innocent and innocuous of stories about him to Randolf, hoping that he might not even notice them. She had hoped he wouldn't even pay attention, with his history as a driver and frequent press clippings. That whole time in their relationship, her heart had thumped in her chest as if on the verge of a heart attack.

Freddie had found out. It turned out he cared... a lot. After he ended their relationship in one sudden and heartbreaking conversation, she had felt cheated. This had been her own doing, sure. But she had specifically given Randolph stories that were so blasé, so uninteresting and undetailed, couldn't he understand that she was protecting him in her own way? Hadn't she at least deserved a second chance? Violet laughed even thinking about it. Second chances never happened. That whole idea was a fairytale.

The gelato-colored buildings surrounding her appeared to dullen as she sat alone at that wrought iron patio table for two. Monaco was a gallery of her happiest and most painful memories, and the landscape a blended mosaic of her wins and losses.

She was marrying a former F1 driver, just as she had dreamt of. She didn't have to write about it anymore. *But I still want to.*

Yanic Blitzgrav emerged when Violet most needed someone. Milking her connection with Randolph, she managed to befriend a couple of socialites who relished the sight of their names in the papers. Maybe they simply didn't care to credit her, but Violet's new 'friends' seemed unaware of her contribution to their publicity.

At one party, Violet recognized Yanic right away. Violet's seductive assertiveness scored her a date by the evening's end. This was her second chance, and she wouldn't repeat her mistakes. Yanic was doting, and he loved Violet more than anything. Violet couldn't understand why.

She shuddered thinking about the money she could make with Yanic's details but that was a door she had cemented shut. There was far more money in store for the woman who kept his secrets.

An inkling of a thought popped into her mind. Freddie already hated her guts. Besides, all of that media attention and spotlight shed on him had done his brand wonders: she knew for a fact that he had profited from fans buying his old paraphernalia from which he still received a cut. Although he wasn't a fan of the eyes on him, having those headlines hadn't been *all* bad. Besides, his life was perfect. Him and his *perfect* Charlotte. Neither of them seemed to have a care in the world. They had their perfect lives and it looked like they were rekindling their romance right where they had left off. She remembered a whole decade earlier watching them from afar in the hallways as that couple in high school who seemed like they had it all figured out.

Heading back to her apartment, she mentally calculated how much in commission she would make from promoting a new collection from a nearby fashion retailer. But that payment wouldn't arrive for at least a few weeks. She bit down on her lip so hard that she came close to puncturing the delicate skin. She only had one month's left of rent to pay before her wedding. Then, she wouldn't have to worry anymore. She just had one month's rent left. Maybe she just wouldn't pay it.

Thinking back to her conversation with Charlotte, she was reeling. There was a certain optic to Freddie and Charlotte reuniting their love after all this time. It didn't feel fair that some people just seemed to have it all so easily.

Grabbing her phone from her handbag, she shot Randolph a text message.

I have a possible story. Need to investigate but could be a big deal. Fixed price?

Almost immediately, Randolph replied. *For anyone else, no. For you, sure. If you deliver.*

Violet felt a wave of relief. This would be it: her last and final bit of gossip sold to Randolph. The idea of her bank account being back in the positives filled with a kind of comfort she wished that it didn't. And since this was going to be her last story she sold, it didn't quite matter if all the details weren't totally and fully aligned, right? After all, what was one more little headline for Freddie Ridgeport?

TEN
Freddie

Freddie waited in the lobby of Le Soleil, tapping his foot against the marble lobby floor. He was used to being a pole sitter, being in first place after qualifying, but right now he wasn't so sure of his position. There was a kind looking young man who peered up at him occasionally from the marble-clad desk, but had said nothing to him, after calling up to the Levant apartment to let them know their guests had arrived. Uncertainty pulsed through his veins, a thin line developing between his brows as he fiddled with his phone. The last time he had been in this atrium, he had left broken-hearted and confused. Surely that wouldn't happen a second him. It couldn't. He hated losing. Pushing the thought of potentially losing twice from his mind, he hyped himself up.

I'm Freddie Ridgeport. I can do anything.

His own apartment wasn't far from Le Soleil, but over the years, he had avoided the block where Charlotte and her grandmother had lived. He really didn't like reliving bad times. Passing by simply filled him with too many memories, mostly of his heartbreak, failure, and embarrassment. For his own self-preservation, he avoided it like a pothole. But even the good memories had brought pain as he struggled to understand what had happened. As a result, he just tried not to think about Charlotte, her grandmother, or Le Soleil at all. That strategy hadn't worked as well as he had hoped.

It felt odd to be right back in the place where they had left off. Back then, he had no idea how he was going to get through it. He had felt tormented by anger, frightened by sadness, and nearly driven mad with questions. Over time, these emotions had softened; or rather, avoidance of them had played a pretty powerful role. No one could live with that much intensity bubbling within them for too long. And it was impossible to feel the pain if it wasn't given attention, Freddie had reasoned with himself.

Perhaps that was why he had dived into racing like never before. It was the perfect outlet to feel everything in as safe of an environment as he had at the time. Racing was the all-time distraction. A sport where he was so focused, that demanded all of his attention, which consumed every minute of his life. And Freddie would tell anyone that racing certainly wasn't always safe, so he had to be on the lookout for danger... including of the heartbreaking variety.

Now that he was back at Le Soleil, he was still confused. But, his heart felt less wrenched from his chest. He now felt nervous for a different reason. It was almost laughable how predictable he felt he had become since his goal now was the same as way back then: he was going to win Charlotte back.

It all felt crystal clear to him. She had finally returned, right when he retired and finally had time for a real, proper relationship. He peered down at Nicholas, who was picking at a scab on his knuckle.

Was this kid going to ruin his chances of being with Charlotte?

"Stop that," he said, grimacing as he looked away from the kid's hand. Even though he had gone through his fair share of scrapes and bruises, Freddie absolutely loathed blood. Or rather, he had a hard time remaining conscious when he saw it. He had fainted once seeing a surgery on TV, never told anyone about it, and avoided it at all costs.

"But there's nothing else to do," Nicholas griped. "I'm bored."

"Count backwards from a thousand," Freddie suggested.

He checked his watch. Surely it couldn't be too much longer.

He was going to really wow her that evening and he felt the same kind of anticipation he got before a race: he had to win. That is, if she was available and interested. He wasn't about to try to break up a marriage. A glimmer of hope bubbled within him, but he dared not get too excited. A woman like Charlotte surely had many men after her. But he wasn't just any man. He was Freddie Ridgeport.

He supposed that at least he wasn't entirely alone this time, which could be seen as a pro or con depending on who was assessing the situation.

Nicholas sat on the white leather sofa beside him. The kid was counting down from a thousand, like Freddie had suggested, but was doing it aloud, which wasn't at all what Freddie had in mind. It turned out that when he wasn't grieving, Nicholas was quite the chatterbox. Freddie was glad to see Nicholas wasn't on the verge of a breakdown; but it certainly hadn't been the romantic, subtle and private meeting he had hoped for. Most people would anticipate that bringing along a chatterbox nine-year-old who couldn't stop thinking or talking about cars might dampen the romance. Freddie was most definitely one of those people. He would have to work extra-hard to make up for it.

And for Nicholas, it was *all* about cars and racing right now. Luckily, it made for an easy, unforced conversation between the two of them. Freddie could reply to the kid without much thought, half-engaged in the conversation and half-stuck in his own mind. It was great that the kid seemed to be coming out of his shell, but did it have to be so *loud*? He wished he could have a moment to himself to gain composure. This certainly wasn't how he had expected to pick up Charlotte—with a nine-year-old in the backseat of his Ferrari.

"Eight-hundred and sixty two... eight-hundred and sixty one..." Nicholas stopped mid-count. "Can I offer you a piece of advice?"

This had ought to be amusing. "Sure. What have you got for me?"

"Don't try to be too showoff*y*."

"Showoff*y*?"

"Yeah, like don't try too hard to impress her. Women don't like that."

Freddie bit down a scoff. "And how do you know what women like?"

"I read it in one of your magazines. You have all of those men's magazines everywhere. Thought I would take a browse. You don't apply a lot of the principles from them, you know. You haven't feng shui*ed* the bathroom yet either, which another article suggests."

"Yeah, well, I think the bathroom looks just fine."

As Nicholas went back to counting, Freddie made a mental note. Was Nicholas right? Should he scale back his showing off?

Checking his watch for what felt like the hundredth time, a ripple of nervousness ran through him. The hairs on his tanned forearms stood on end. What if she wasn't going to show up. How would he ever get over it? Let alone get over the embarrassment? He had waited in that lobby how many times before only to leave alone...*again*?

But there was something even more important about talking to Charlotte than rekindling romance. Charlotte was the only person, apart from Christian and the teachers at Nicholas' school, who knew that he had taken Nicholas on and was now his legal guardian. Would Charlotte be able to be discreet? Of course, it wasn't a secret. But he knew how quickly gossip could spread. Eventually, everyone would know, but for now he was keeping things as under wraps as could be. He wanted to shield Nicholas from as much scandal as possible. Especially since his name had been the tabloid headlines only a short while earlier. He knew how angry he had gotten then; he couldn't imagine how he would feel if Nicholas' information was leaked to the press.

The elevator doors opened and out walked Charlotte, looking like an angel in a creamy white dress that clung to her every curve. Freddie shook his head in astonishment. There was something about her that was addictive. She certainly appeared to be worth waiting for. Now, he still felt nervous but this time it was a different kind. His eyes were locked on hers; they were like magnets as their bodies drew closer. Feeling entirely electric, the chemistry between them was undeniable. Surely she couldn't have a boyfriend or husband.

She leaned in for a hug. Clearly she had gotten used to American customs. Freddie certainly didn't mind. "Nice to see you," she said, her face dangerously close to his. If he wanted to, he could kiss her. He wouldn't. He *couldn't.* That would ruin everything.

"And you," he replied, taking her hands in his. Her dainty hands felt right in his. He noticed her cuticles, frayed, and said nothing. Clearly an old habit she hadn't forgotten. She had bitten her nails ceaselessly while the two of them were together, particularly around the end of their relationship. *Was she stressed now?*

Then he watched as Charlotte's gaze flickered to Nicholas, who had jumped up to his feet and beamed at Charlotte with a wide smile. If she was upset, she hid it well.

"Hi Nicholas," Charlotte said pointedly as she took a step back, a smirk forming on her full mouth.

"Hi Charlotte," Nicholas replied politely. "I can't wait to go to the racetrack tonight. Thank you so much for taking me. You look beautiful this evening, might I add."

Freddie rolled his eyes. It was just his luck that the kid would have the first word. But now this kid was upstaging him. Charlotte's eyes whipped back to Freddie, and he gave an apologetic shrug. So much for Nicholas not being much of a distraction.

He cleared his throat. "What Nicholas means is that we thought we would go to the racetrack *quickly* and then have a really wonderful dinner," Freddie jumped in, talking more rapidly than normal. He began to feel hot and his shirt collar began to feel tight. "And yes, you do look especially beautiful this evening," he added. Why was he *so* nervous? Normally he was exceptional at talking to women. A year earlier, he would have listed it as his second best skill, right after racing cars that is.

Charlotte blinked as she looked from him to Nicholas and back to him. For an instant, his heart dropped as he anticipated that she might say no. But relief flooded him as her face broke into a smile, the kind she reserved for a select few. All of his worry melted.

"You're dripping," Nicholas said, pointing to a bead of sweat that trickled down Freddie's forehead.

Freddie wiped it away savagely. "No, I'm not," he growled. "I mean, why don't we get going?"

Charlotte stifled a giggle.

Nicholas smiled as well, a genuine happy smile back to them both.

Freddie forced a smile too, although inside he was a nervous wreck. *This is going to be okay*, he told himself. *What could go wrong?*

Freddie buckled himself into a go-kart. Charlotte was strapping on a helmet beside him. Nicholas was proudly sitting in the go-kart ahead of them. Kids were screaming all around, the sound reverberating and echoing off the walls.

"Are you sure this is safe?" Charlotte asked tentatively. From beneath her confident veneer, Freddie was certain he could detect a hint of panic.

"You'll have fun," Freddie said, trying to inject the right note of enthusiasm into his tone—not enough to make it seem like this was his plan all along, but not so little that he sounded like a buzz kill.

He had *told* Nicholas that the go-karting would be for him and him alone. Before the two of them had left that evening, he had gone at length to explain to the kid that him and Charlotte needed their private time to talk while he raced *alone* on the track. It would be a perfect compromise, Freddie had thought.

Although the drive to MonacoGo from Le Soleil was only a few minutes, Nicholas seemed even chattier around Charlotte. To Freddie's surprise, Charlotte had beleaguered Nicholas with questions, which the kid had happily answered. Of course, Charlotte was kind. She would never snub a child; especially one as engaging as Nicholas. Freddie was surprised he had learned a few things just from listening to the two of them chat. Who knew that Nicholas' favorite food was pizza or that he had a crush on a girl named Miranda in his class? Initially, Freddie had wanted to talk as much as he could with Charlotte but just being in her presence, witnessing how she connected and communicated with Nicholas, was *almost* better. She seemed to have a knack with kids.

The second that they had arrived at the karting track, Nicholas had excitedly taken Charlotte's hand and insisted that she give it a try. Freddie wanted to protest, but what ground did he have to stand on? Charlotte had looked delighted at the idea.

"It's like flying, Charlotte," he said for the millionth time that day. "You *have* to try it."

So far, Freddie had barely gotten in a word between Nicholas and Charlotte. Now, he was sitting beside Charlotte but they each had their helmets on. It was difficult to hear her above the roar of the engines. Ahead of them, Nicholas started first and zoomed off, hooting and hollering.

It took everything in him not to slam his right foot onto the pedal and give that go-kart the ride of its life. Restraining himself and not chasing after Nicholas proved to be harder than he thought. He waited with Charlotte as she acclimatized herself to the go-kart. He wanted to *win*. He wanted to show off to Charlotte. She wasn't just out on a date with anyone—she was with a three-time World Champion. He would show her just how talented he was. He revved his engine.

"You'll stick close to me, right?" Charlotte asked.

Nicholas' words rang through his mind. *Don't be a showoff.* Freddie nodded, his face not matching his agreement. "Right, yes, of course. I'll be right here."

As the two of them started their engines, he could hear Charlotte screaming in delight as they took off simultaneously.

Pace yourself, Freddie told himself. She looked back at him with a grin and Freddie gave her the thumbs up. A kid half his age lapped them. He fought against the urge to speed. He was going to have to suppress every instinct in his body.

All around the track, lap after lap, Charlotte was screaming out in excitement. Freddie couldn't stop smiling from underneath his helmet, even if he was doing the slowest lap he had ever driven in his entire life. If that didn't prove how happy he was to see Charlotte having a good time, he didn't know what else would. He still grimaced whenever they were lapped. Losing was no fun at all. Charlotte looked at him and her face, the picture of joy, was undoubtedly the best win. She drove slowly and carefully, making conservative turns and exercising good judgment. But as they pulled off to finish, it was the freest expression he had ever seen on her. Not an ounce of composure on that smiling, beaming, excited face.

He motioned for them to pull off to the side.

"Now I get why you just *had* to become a racecar driver," she said to him as she took off her helmet. Her cheeks were flushed, her hair a mess, and she had never looked happier.

Freddie wasn't about to correct her that driving a Formula One car was much, *much* more fun, but he held off. *Don't be a showoff.* He was just happy to see her having fun. It turned out that racing was a hit. It was all thanks to Nicholas. The kid pulled up behind them, grinding his engine to a stop, looking even happier than Charlotte. Nicholas seemed to be assessing Charlotte's expression as he took off his helmet, just as Freddie had.

"I knew you'd love it," Nicholas said brightly, as if he had known Charlotte his whole life. "We should start a racing team!"

Freddie laughed good naturedly at what he thought was Nicholas' joke, but Charlotte looked gravely serious as she nodded.

"I would like that," she said. "I'll be on your racing team, Nicholas."

Nicholas beamed in return.

The three of them handed in their helmets and convened outside as they grabbed their respective belongings. Freddie checked his watch. They had just enough time to get to Vincenzo's, an impeccable Italian restaurant right on the Sea where he had snagged a waterfront table. They would be dining al fresco with the sea mist on their faces and award-winning Italian food on their plates. He couldn't think of anything more romantic; except, of course, if the reservation was made for two instead of three.

"I'm starving," Nicholas said, after they had given back all of their protective gear.

"Hey, didn't you say your favorite food is pizza?" Charlotte asked, turning to Nicholas.

Nicholas' face lit up, as if he already knew what was coming his way. "Sure is."

"Well, why don't we grab pizza? Freddie, you said you had wanted to grab dinner after this, isn't that right?"

Freddie forced a smile. He was already grieving the crab and asparagus appetizer that he had planned on ordering from Vincenzo's. Nothing about tonight was going according to plan. He was just going to have to go with the flow of things that evening.

"Sounds good to me," he managed. Inside, he was thinking about the lemon and truffle aioli that paired perfectly with the salmon, the wine, and the oysters he had planned to order. Silently, he willed for Nicholas or Charlotte to change their minds about pizza, but he knew he was undoubtedly going to be eating pizza that night.

Not that he had anything against pizza, of course. He ate it most nights. But tonight was supposed to be special.

Nothing was turning out for Freddie like he had expected. His plans—foiled. His vision for the night—hilariously different than anything he could have expected. But somehow, while looking from Nicholas' eager face to Charlotte, he knew he had to surrender all control. And somehow everything had turned out okay. Not just okay, *brilliant.* Charlotte had enjoyed herself so much at MonacoGo; it was almost like he got a glimpse into her soul that few had the opportunity to. The carefree, relaxed, no composure version of the girl he had loved for so long.

Tonight, all plans were out the window. So far, it had worked for him. He wasn't in the driver's seat anymore. Not in the slightest. He was taking the backseat. Usually, this bothered him so much he tried to get out of the car. Being driven was *the worst.* But tonight, for some reason, he didn't mind it at all. Tonight Charlotte was in the driver's seat, Nicholas was the passenger, and he would just have to enjoy their company from the backseat. It seemed like a fine idea.

"Where should we go?" Nicholas asked as they buckled into Freddie's Ferrari.

"Hmm..." Charlotte bemused aloud. "I don't know. Why don't we just see what looks good? Maybe drive around a bit?"

Freddie nodded, a slow smile forming on his face. "Okay, he said. I'll drive. You just tell me when to stop."

Charlotte nodded and he cranked up the tunes to his favorite music, which came blaring over the sound system. Nicholas began to sing the lyrics. Freddie flinched. Nicholas sang loud and off-key.

"*And when they sayyyyyyyyyy, it's just another dayyyyyyy...*" Nicholas was giving it his all.

Freddie's heart skipped a beat, thinking about what Charlotte must be thinking. And then he heard the harmony.

"*They're in love anywayyyyyyyy,*" Charlotte sung, as if competing with Nicholas for who could sing more off-key.

Freddie beamed. He wasn't much of a singer. He hummed along to the tune.

Perhaps a special night had nothing to do with the plans, Freddie wondered. Instead of going full throttle, he was lifting up the brake and coasting. Maybe he didn't need to try so hard. Perhaps the only thing that made an evening special was entirely dependent on the people that it was shared with. In his case, with Charlotte and *even* Nicholas by his side, he was certain that it was a *very* special night indeed.

ELEVEN
Charlotte

Charlotte sipped a cup of tea at midnight with a trembling hand. She felt electric, unable to sleep. That had been more than a fact-finding mission. That was the best night of her life. It was more than she could ever have hoped for.

A warm glow seemed to have overcome her ever since she arrived home, soothing a decade old wound. She knew she wasn't going to fall asleep that night. Who in their right mind would be able to after an evening like that? Ever since Freddie had dropped her off hours before, she mentally replayed the events over and over again in her mind.

It had been perfect. The kind of evening she would have never thought possible in her wildest dreams. Freddie, Nicholas—*Nicholas*. Her baby boy, who was not such a baby anymore. She wasn't even teary eyed, like she usually became when she thought about him too much. Charlotte felt a swoop of joy. But she worried about the inevitable guilt that would soon follow.

She had just met her son. He had no idea of her true identity. To him, she was that cool lady Charlotte who seemed to like everything he did. At least, that's what she expected that he thought of her.

She had tried all evening to soak up every moment, to give him the most fun and perfect evening too. Feelings of shame, guilt, sorrow *should* have been pumping through her veins full throttle, but truthfully, Charlotte felt nothing but joy as she lay in her bed with her eyes wide open, staring at her ceiling. Replaying the night they just had, Charlotte grinned. How that evening carried such profoundly different meanings for them all.

Freddie's obvious affection for her hadn't escaped Charlotte's observation. Her heart swelled, recalling the way he had looked in her direction. The way that he had driven beside her on that racetrack to make sure she enjoyed herself. Most importantly, Charlotte was struck by how Freddie treated Nicholas. After all, he had just adopted this boy, unbeknownst to him his biological son. Neither of them knew the truth. Easily, it could have been a recipe for friction, conflict, frustration. Charlotte observed nothing but patience from Freddie, and he looked at Nicholas with tenderness and guarded him with a sense of protection. Already, she could see him taking on a fatherly role, even though he had no idea his true role as a father.

That evening, Charlotte had gotten to live out her secret fantasy that she knew could never come true. It was like they were a real family. *A real family.* It was nothing like she had experienced with her own family growing up—with her emotionally unstable mother and absentee father. No, this was the real deal. At least, for that one night.

This is just temporary, she reminded herself. *Don't get too attached.*

Too late.

"Knock, knock?" her mémé asked, opening the door to her bedroom slightly. "Sorry, I didn't mean to startle you."

"That's all right."

"How did your evening go?"

Her mémé's voice, hopeful and concerned simultaneously, was the grounding force she felt that she needed.

"Perfect," Charlotte said, biting down a smile.

Her mémé came and sat down on her bed, just as she had to comfort Charlotte so many times in her early life. "I cannot believe I didn't know," her mémé said, shaking her head. "I just cannot believe it."

Charlotte shrugged. "You fell. You had your surgery. You haven't left your house," she said with a strangled laugh. "It makes sense you wouldn't have heard that Freddie had adopted Nicholas."

"Perhaps. But I know everything about this country," her mémé said with resolve. "It's possible I'm losing my spark."

"Don't say that, mémé," Charlotte pleaded. "I get the feeling that Freddie has been trying to keep this under wraps. I don't think he wants the whole world to know. At least, that's the impression I get."

"Why do you say that?" her mémé asked with raised eyebrows.

"Well, I looked it up online," Charlotte admitted. "There's nothing about 'F1 racer Freddie Ridgeport adopting a son'. No news articles. Nothing like that. But there's tons of other stuff way more menial. News articles with photos about him on vacation, retiring from racing…"

"Well, that makes me feel a tad better," her mémé said, her eyes brightening again. "Now what are you going to do next?" her mémé continued in a kind but firm tone. "Are you going to see them again?"

Charlotte hugged her knees into her chest, wanting to forget about the future entirely and simply relish in the evening. It had been so perfect, after all. "I don't know," she managed. "I've gotten the information that I needed. Nicholas is in good hands. The *best* hands. I know I should bow out now."

With a sigh, her mémé gently touched Charlotte's cheek. "I know this is hard for you, *mon cherie*, but just think how much harder it will be if you continue to see them. Freddie is still in love with you, surely you've gathered that much. I've seen the way he still looks at me at the market when we run into one another from time to time, with equal parts fear, curiosity, and affection. He misses you. He always had. He always will."

Charlotte felt herself blushing furiously. "Oh, well, I don't know about that…" she managed, but her voice felt tight and shaky. Her mémé knew everything.

"Well, I'm not going to tell you how to live your life, but I'll leave you with this: tread carefully, my darling. There has been more than enough heartbreak in this family. I don't want to see you, or those two boys, hurt anymore."

Charlotte nodded as her mémé bid her goodnight and slipped out of her bedroom, leaving her feeling more confused about what she should do than ever. The wise decision would have been to leave them alone. Her presence complicated everything.

Maybe you can help. The thought sprang to her mind like a loose bolt becoming unhinged. *You can see how they're doing at home. You can offer some parenting advice. You. Can. Help.*

The idea made Charlotte feel just a teensy bit giddy. Before she had actually met with Freddie and her dear Nicholas face-to-face, she thought that she could have that *one* evening and let things be. That had been her plan. One meeting and then that would be it. She had thought that the evening would settle her curiosity. It would allow her to determine with one-hundred-percent crystal clear certainty that Nicholas was okay, that Freddie was equipped for what he had signed up for, and maybe even reconcile the guilt in her heart that she had made the right decision all those years earlier. Now that she had met Nicholas, how could she leave it at just one visit?

So far, she felt that Nicholas had a very happy life before his parents' death; but even still, Freddie seemed to be taking to the new role like a fish in water.

Still, everyone needed help from time to time. Couldn't she see them once more? *Maybe* twice? She could drop off some parenting books for Freddie, as she was certain he was flying by the seed of his pants as he always did, some toys for Nicholas, and she could also do a bit of prodding to get a better understanding of how Nicholas was faring psychologically. Maybe she could recommend a good psychologist.

Perhaps I need one myself.

A stab of frustration at the Stefano's came out of nowhere. Wasn't it strange that the Stefanos had chosen Freddie? Hadn't they known how it would complicate matters? What if Freddie hadn't been ready to be a father? She had arranged for everything to be neat and clean. This situation was a giant mess. Still, she would do her best to clean it up before she bid them farewell.

She had always wondered what Nicholas would be like. Now she had met him. She saw a glimpse into his beautiful little soul. His dimples, his face, his personality—he was perfect. That original plan of saying goodbye to them was now impossible. Her mémé's words rang through her mind but she pushed them back. *She could help.* One more visit, *maybe* two at the most, just to help Freddie sort things out. Then, she would be gone before any emotions got in the way.

She didn't want anyone to get hurt. She would have to be incredibly careful. But she couldn't miss out on any more time. Those few visits would be all she needed to soak up every bit of Nicholas and ensure he was all right. After all, she still had a few weeks left to remain in Monaco and help her mémé. No flights had been booked home yet, and her school principal had told her to take all the time that she had needed; according to the email they had sent to her, a suitable substitute was found who was willing to stay on for however long was needed.

For the last ten years, she had been oversteering. Perhaps it was time to understeer.

A frisson of delight washed over her. She could stay in Monaco for however long she wanted. Even if she wouldn't be in touch with them, she could keep a surreptitious eye out for them. *One or two more visits with Freddie and Nicholas wouldn't be too bad. In fact, it was probably a sage idea.*

Besides, she had only just met Nicholas. How could she walk away from him so quickly? It took more than one meeting to get to know someone. She would have to see him at least two more times to fully ensure he was faring well. And *Freddie.* She wished that her heart hadn't fluttered when she had seen him. She wished that her cheeks hadn't felt hot when he had smiled in her direction. There must be something she could offer them they didn't already have—she would need to stop off to buy some books and toys for Nicholas in the morning. And read a parenting book quickly so she could bestow Freddie with some maternal wisdom. Besides, she wasn't going to stay in Monaco forever. She would simply spend more time with the two of them, easing her conscience and filling her heart with healing. And then she would leave and head back to New York.

How could anything bad come from that?

TWELVE
Freddie

A racecar is just a fast car until you pit it against a bunch of other fast cars. That's when the race begins. Some people love the speed but hate the competition. Some love the competition and are terrified of the speed. You need both to be a successful F1 driver.

Nicholas had both.

Freddie was chuffed that he had instantly recognized those traits in Nicholas, right from the moment that he stepped into that go-kart. There was a certain *hunger* for winning that couldn't be taught. Natural talent paired with this instinct to completely crush your opponent was a deadly combination. Being friendly and affable off the track were merely a bonus. Nicholas certainly seemed to have it all.

"Can you pass me another croissant?" Nicholas asked, rubbing the sleep out of his eye.

It was a talent to see the raw potential a nine-year-old had; especially when Freddie had seen Nicholas' full-spectrum, from his sleepy-morning-self to his grieving-self to his racing-self. Freddie struggled to see the kid's potential right now but he knew that beneath that relaxed veneer was a sleeping lion, ready to be unleashed on the track.

"You want to go to the grid today, champ?" Freddie asked

hopefully. He knew that Nicholas would say yes. Truthfully, it was the first time since his retirement that Freddie felt truly excited about something—except for Charlotte Levant, of course. He realized how much he missed being around that world. He missed the thrill. Having someone to root for made it so much sweeter.

He felt hopeful about Nicholas' future when he saw him in that kart. Having something to look forward to was imperative in life. After becoming an orphan and living in a new person's house, Freddie imagined that Nicholas hadn't had much to look forward to before getting into that go-kart. Now, that kid had a world of hope.

If he wanted it, that was.

Charlotte and Nicholas had hit it off better than he could have ever expected the night before. From his memory of her ten years earlier, she was always polite. No one *dis*liked her. But she was reserved and aloof. For many people, she was hard to get to know. When she let someone into her private world, there was a sense of privilege that came with it. She didn't allow just anyone in.

But that couldn't have been further from the Charlotte he had seen last night. Yes, there was still the same element of elegance and reservation about her. But as she had stuffed her face with pizza sitting along the pier, laughing until her nose scrunched up at Nicholas' jokes and his own stories about his early racing gaffes, it seemed Charlotte had transformed into a fuller, happier version of herself. As she had laughed at one of Nicholas' jokes, bent over at her waist from laughter and choking on her pizza, Freddie realized that he was, without a doubt, still in love with this woman.

And from the way that she had brushed his arm with her fingertips after saying goodbye, her total and complete acceptance of his new situation with Nicholas, and how she had looked at him with crinkled and smiling eyes, he thought that she might love him too.

Magnetic, radiant, and bubbling over with joy—it was only morning but he needed to see Charlotte again. He hadn't stopped thinking about her since he dropped her off. Burning questions still ate him up inside, ones that he hadn't gotten a chance to ask her. Why had she left? What had happened ten years ago? Why hadn't she reached out to him all of those years? Why was she back now? He had planned to ask her all of those things over dinner, and then some. But it just hadn't been the right time. Especially at a busy pizzeria where they had sat next to a family of tourists. He needed to see her again. It seemed that Nicholas had taken a shine to her as well.

"Is Charlotte going to be there?" Nicholas asked, a mouthful of crumbs spilling out of his mouth.

"I suppose it wouldn't hurt to ask if she's around," Freddie mused aloud, wondering if it seemed too cloying to ask her out a second day in a row. His feelings for Charlotte had been jumpstarted. But then again, they had waited ten years for this. Who knew when the opportunity would come again? If she slipped through his fingertips like sand, he would never forgive himself.

Stagnant, relaxed, *laissez-faire* were not words that Freddie would have ever used to describe himself. Since the age of sixteen, he had a fire that burned inside of him, fuelling his desire to get out on the track and *win*. It wasn't as simple as saying that he was retired to turn off that ignition deep within his soul.

Although he had relished in his time off for the first few days, Freddie had woken up to that gorgeous Monaco view during his retirement and wondered what he was going to do with his day. He had hated not having a plan. He despised not having intention. Retirement just didn't seem to fit as snugly as he had hoped. There were no competitions to train for, no problems with his racing team to navigate, no pressing meetings, no flights to catch. It was just him and his mind and a lot of empty time. Enter Nicholas three months earlier—and that empty time became filled with more overwhelm, uncertainty and confusion than he had ever faced. How was he going to help this kid? *Could* he even help this kid? Why on Earth had the Stefanos chosen him to raise their son? Why? Why? *Why?*

Now, he had an inkling of excitement about racing coming back to him. He felt a glimmer of confidence about his ability to help Nicholas. That same fire in his core, the one that had fuelled him to wake up early, compete through colds and jet lag, was returning. He saw that same fire in Nicholas, and it dawned on him that perhaps this was why the Stefanos had chosen him in the first place. Maybe they had seen something in him that he hadn't seen in himself; he certainly had a gift when it came to building and growing that inner fire.

"Come on, get dressed," Freddie said to Nicholas. He pushed back all of his worries as he shot off a quick text to Charlotte, asking her to meet them at MonacoGo if she was free. Racing against the best drivers in the world? He didn't flinch. But his heart was pounding and he felt all hot and flushed the moment he had pressed send.

"You're the best," Nicholas said as he jumped up, pumping his fist in the air.

Freddie wished that he could have recorded that moment. All the anxiety from before seemed to dissipate. Silently, he willed for the universe to keep sending him all of this good luck. Nicholas sure seemed to bring a lot of luck to him.

"First one in and last one out," Freddie explained to Nicholas, trying to impart some expert wisdom. "That's the key to success."

"Unless you're actually racing," Nicholas added thoughtfully. "Then you'd be penalized for an early start. Plus, you'd come in last."

Freddie sucked his teeth. "Right, well, why don't you hurry up before I change my mind?"

It always seemed to be that just as things were aligning perfectly, life had a way of shaking things up. Charlotte had agreed to meet them at the grid. Nicholas was pumped and he was elated. He stood on the sidelines and waved the kid off as he stood along the edge of the track on his own when he heard a familiar voice.

"Frederick?"

The hairs on the back of his neck stood on end. Only one person called him by that name, even though she knew he hated it. To her, it made him sound more like the "racing royalty" that he was, which had been her words... not his. And Freddie couldn't stand it.

He turned and gave an inward shudder. Just as he thought,

Violet MacIntyre was walking towards him with a wide grin, as if their last conversation hadn't been her spewing hateful words towards him after he had broken things off. Somehow, he had managed to avoid her in that small country in the months since he had ended things. He had even gone so far as to wonder if she had moved. Apparently not.

His heart sank. Of all the times for his ex-girlfriend to show up, now just wasn't it. Plus, Violet wasn't exactly what one could call *discreet.* What she saw, she reported to everyone and anyone who would listen to her. In the best of times, it made her gregarious, playful, and fun to be around. In the worst of times, it made her untrustworthy. He really didn't want to explain the whole Nicholas situation to her, let alone have to introduce her to Charlotte. If there was anyone who would have a million questions, and actually ask them, it was Violet.

Freddie often prided himself on making the right decisions early on in his life. To the best of his ability, he had navigated his early fame and success as well as he could. But like any human, there were certain paths that Freddie wished he had never gone down. Often, he learned from his mistakes quickly and chose not to revisit those paths in his life, refusing to make the same error twice. Violet was one of those errors. Freddie had found that years worth of good decisions could be unwound with one bad choice. For him, that one choice had been to trust Violet in their yearlong relationship together. He had foolishly trusted her and disclosed to her details about his troubled childhood and pained breakup with Charlotte Levant. He had even cried on her shoulder one night, a memory he would pay a million euros to take back.

He shuddered upon seeing Violet again, remembering how silly he was to think that he had finally found love. A love that would stick around. What he had really was a leech. Sometimes, they look the same to a fragile heart. She had fast-tracked him to burnout.

Freddie gave Violet a tight-lipped smile, hoping that she would take the hint and stay where she was. He was beyond trying to pretend to sweep it all under the rug. She had betrayed him, broken his trust, and hurt him beyond repair. But Violet was her usual self today—

smiling at him as if nothing bad had happened. She had a way of compartmentalizing her actions and pretended like nothing was wrong most of the time. How on Earth had he remained in a relationship with her for so long?

"What, you're not even going to say hi?" Violet teased, walking up to him and stopped so close that he could smell her familiar perfume. He used to love that scent. Now, he wanted nothing more than to be six-feet away from her.

"Why are you here, Violet? Are you here to talk? Because like I said the last time—"

"—I'm here to watch Pierre. He's Yanic's son. You know Yanic Blitzgrav?"

"Yes, I know Yanic," Freddie said, taking pity on the poor man whose heart she was now toying with. Freddie knew Yanic. He was another retired race car driver in Monaco who had won Le Mans a decade earlier before retiring. Yanic was a nice guy. Surely he had no idea who he was dealing with.

Violet had popped up in multiple places that Freddie frequented in the weeks following his breakup with her. She had suddenly been at his favorite coffee shop, his favorite restaurant, his running route... Monaco was small but not *that* small. But in recent months he hadn't seen her at all. It made sense: she was probably spending all of her time in Yanic's yacht. Since Freddie had a boat of his own, he had actually run into Yanic about six months earlier at the marina, and Yanic had told him all about it. Yanic was a nice guy, but he seemed to obsess over material objects. Freddie had ducked out of the conversation after the ten-minute mark when Yanic had steered the conversation towards his latest acquisition: his car. Presumably this conversation had been before he had met Violet, otherwise he would have known.

"Yes, it's a small world, isn't it? Well, I've been seeing Yanic for months now. It's getting serious," she added with a wink. "I'm here watching his son," she continued, gesturing vaguely towards the track.

Freddie tried to conceal his laughter with a cough. Violet?

Taking care of a kid? Violet cared about one person and one person alone: herself.

"And where is this child who you're supposedly watching?"

Violet looked around, her eyes dashing to all corners of the room. "Somewhere here," she managed, her eyes never managing to stay in one spot for too long. "Doesn't matter. But since you brought it up, speaking of children, the real question is I'm dying to know is who is this child who *you're* here with? Are you babysitting?" she asked, poking him in the chest.

Freddie had worked hard to keep the details of Nicholas' life under wraps. Things were already tough enough for the kid without the weight of everyone's judgment upon him. Freddie knew first hand just how hard it was to have one's personal life under scrutiny. And he was an adult with years worth of media training behind him. He was doing the best he could, and he didn't need prying eyes making things harder. Besides, Violet was the last person he would tell. Let people speculate. But Freddie wasn't about to start tattling the news to everyone.

"I'm afraid it's not a very interesting story," Freddie said wryly, turning to face the grid once again. He had given up a few minutes of his attention to Violet, which had taken away from his time watching Nicholas. That was more than enough time.

"Oh, I don't know about that," she prodded.

"Shoot," Freddie said, looking down at his watch. "I've got a call scheduled. Sorry to cut our chat short," he fibbed on both accounts. He had learned that the bigger a deal he made of something, the more Violet pried. He thought he had done a pretty good job at covering his tracks.

As Violet opened her mouth to speak, he heard another familiar voice calling out from nearby.

"Go Nicholas! Go Nicholas!"

From the corner of his eye, he saw Charlotte walking to where he was standing, cheering for Nicholas the whole way. His heart leapt. She had come.

The kid zoomed by them again, hooting and hollering.

Nicholas sounded how Freddie felt. A swooping sensation overcame him as she walked towards him. A gauzy scarf was wrapped around her neck as threw her hands in the air, seemingly more enthusiastic than the rest of the parents there. With a head nod to Violet, hoping to signal the end of their conversation, Freddie walked towards Charlotte. She looked radiant as she beamed at Nicholas on the track, her energy infectious as Freddie got nearer.

"He's doing amazing," Charlotte gushed, barely able to tear her eyes off of the racers. Nicholas was racing at an awe-inspiring level. It was hard to believe that this was only his second day on the grid. Clearly Charlotte thought so too. "Do you think he has any idea of how talented he is?"

Nicholas zoomed by them again, shouting in delight so loud that it rivaled the roar of the engines.

"Oh, I think he's got a slight idea," Freddie managed, fighting the urge to tell Charlotte about how he had overheard Nicholas talking to himself in the mirror that morning, pretending that he was being interviewed for being "the fastest and most naturally talented racer in the world". Sometimes, he wished that he had someone to share all of these moments with. They were certainly adding up a lot more quickly than he could have ever expected.

"Look at him," Charlotte pointed out. "Overtaking that kid there. On my way in, I overheard a couple of the parents' over there asking who he is. They were saying they've never seen him here before but were guessing he had trained in Germany? They think he's here to compete," she added with a wink.

Freddie matched Charlotte's grin. "Well, they've got one thing right. He's definitely here to compete."

When things were going so well, life had a way of making it all interesting. He was holding Charlotte's gaze, feeling his heartbeat steadily rising. From the corner of his eye, he watched as Violet let out an exasperated sigh and stormed off. Thank goodness she hadn't made a scene; or worse, began her line of questioning with Charlotte directly. A small thing to be grateful for, but he would take it.

Finally, the two of them were alone. Sure, they were surrounded by parents but at least by this point no one else was within ear shot. It had been the first time that the two of them had any significant period of time together. Their date was incredible. He hadn't been able to think of anything else the night before, replaying moment after moment in his head until he fell asleep. Of course, Nicholas being there was certainly unconventional. But somehow, it had worked. Now, the two of them smiled at each other bashfully. This was the moment to ask her some of those questions that he hadn't been able to ask last night. Questions that had burned in the back of his mind for years, his curiosity slowly eating away at him. Why had she left without saying a word ten years earlier? Where had she been? What had happened? He would never be able to forgive himself if she disappeared again, taking with her the answers to those questions. He had to ask. It was now or never… at least to him.

"You know," she began in a thoughtful tone. "Most parenting experts suggest that you praise the child's effort, not their performance."

"Is that so?"

"And no harsh criticism."

Freddie's eyebrows shot up. "I would never."

"I know, but I remember how hard you used to be on yourself."

Freddie smiled. She remembered. She clearly hadn't forgotten their early years together, especially to remember a detail like that. Had he been hard on himself? He had just been doing what he thought he had to do to win.

He took a deep breath. "Charlotte…" he began, licking his dry lips.

Charlotte looked at him with wide eyes. "Yes?"

Zoooooooooooooooom.

"That kids' amazing!" someone yelled from nearby. "Who is that?"

"Great effort!" Charlotte cheered at the top of her lungs. "You look like you're working really hard!"

Nicholas drove right by them at such a speed that the entire building of MonacoGo seemed to vibrate. Freddie couldn't help but stop his train of thought. His eyes veered from Charlotte's, towards the grid, and a glimmer of pride struck him right when he needed it most. He looked back towards Charlotte and she was grinning at him, shaking her head slowly as if she couldn't believe it. He could barely believe it either. His brain felt foggy. What had he wanted to ask her? Right now, all he wanted to do was celebrate.

Charlotte seemed to have the exact same impulse.

He couldn't ignore that her eyes had dropped to his mouth. His entire body, electrified, was drawn to her with every impulse in his body. The entire crowd around them seemed to fade away into a haze, just as it had when he was racing. Just like back then, he was focused on one thing. Cautiously, he took a step towards her but Charlotte beat him to it.

Her lips met his. Familiar yet different, those full lips, that perfume. He wrapped his arms around her, feeling her heart beating against his own chest, and never wanting to let her go. But Charlotte seemed to have other ideas. She pulled away suddenly, stumbling slightly as if dizzy.

"I'm so sorry, I don't know what came over me..." she fumbled, her cheeks reddening and looking around sheepishly as if to see who had witnessed it. There was a guilty smile upon her face, which he matched.

"No, no, that's more that all right," Freddie said, wishing that they could get back to where they had left off. "That's totally fine…"

"I just... got excited with all that good news. Seeing Nicholas just now. Seeing you… It's brought back a lot." Charlotte said quickly, crossing her arms over her chest.

"Yeah, yeah, me too. That's totally fine," Freddie said, trying to play it off cool. In reality, he could barely believe his good fortune. He wanted to say the right thing. *Anything* to make her kiss him again. He racked his brain for what to say but smiled goofily instead, just like he had after their very first kiss a whole decade earlier. He couldn't help himself. He put his hands in his back pockets, looking down before meeting her eye again.

Charlotte beamed back at him, a slightly guilty expression on her flushed face.

Slowly, the world around them came back into soft focus. The chattering and murmuring of other parents and coaches around them. Had anyone been paying attention to them? Had anyone seen what had happened?

But truthfully, Freddie couldn't care less at that moment. Charlotte had kissed him. She had kissed *him*! Nothing in his entire world could go wrong right now. The two of them stood in front of one another, their chests rising and falling, just like teenagers who had been caught making out on school grounds, sheepish grins covering them both. Right now, the only thing that would make this moment more *perfect* would be if Charlotte kissed him again. He didn't want to overstep his boundary or make her uncomfortable by going for it himself.

A blood-curdling boom rang through MonacoGo, halting all conversations and even the cars on the track. Freddie's heart sank. He knew that sound.

Nicholas.

Their gaze broke as both his and Charlotte's heads swiveled to the grid. A few people had already begun running to the track. The rest of the cars were flagged to pull over and stop. A trail of smoke wafted up from the site of the noise, but through the crowd, Freddie couldn't see who it was.

Panic pulsed through him; his head feeling like it was going to explode. Was Nicholas all right? He ran to get a closer look and his heart dropped into his stomach when he saw the reality. Nicholas' go-kart lay on its side.

Nicholas was lying motionless. No, no, no. No, no, no, no, no. *No.*

All thoughts stopped and his body went straight into dread

mode. Without so much as a thought, Freddie broke the cardinal rule and jumped onto the grid as a few of the go-karts were still being flagged off to the sides, running as fast as his feet would carry him towards where Nicholas was laying. Nicholas was very still. *Make any kind of motion*, Freddie silently willed. Fighting the worst-case scenario thoughts that ran through his mind, every panic-alarm in Freddie's body was going off and he reached Nicholas, beads of perspiration pouring down his face.

"It's going to be okay, it's going to be okay," he murmured to Nicholas, although he knew he was half-saying it for himself as well.

Nicholas was laying half-in the go-kart, half-on the ground. His face was contorted in pain although he wasn't saying anything. His forearm was scraped and a couple beads of blood trickled down his hand.

Freddie averted his gaze, trying to take steady breaths. He could faint right now. *Come on*, he said in his mind to Nicholas. *Be okay*.

"Where does it hurt?" Freddie pleaded, sitting beside the kid. He was quickly joined by a medley of staff and concerned parents. "Don't touch him!" he instructed the others. If it was a broken neck, or a fractured spine, the very worst thing that they could do right now would be to try and move him. Right now, he needed to remain still.

"My arm," Nicholas managed, tears welling in his big innocent eyes.

Freddie didn't say so, but inwardly he breathed a sigh of relief. Nicholas was talking. He was communicating. He was *alive*. If Nicholas weren't in such pain, he would have hugged the life out of him.

"And your head? Did you hit your head? How about your neck or back?"

Nicholas began to move his good arm to his head. "Okay, I think—"

"—Don't move!" Freddie nearly yelled. "Sorry, don't move," he repeated, this time a bit more softly. "You are probably in shock. I just want to make sure that you're safe."

"What's wrong? Is he okay?" Charlotte called. He could hear

her footsteps from behind him and her breaths coming in heaves.

"We need an ambulance," Freddie directed.

"Don't worry," she crouched down beside Nicholas, patting his hand and careful not to move him. "I've already called and they're on their way."

Within what felt like eternity, although only minutes, paramedics assisted Nicholas out of the go-kart, as no one wanted to be the person to potentially worsen his injury. Freddie sat by his side the entire time, beads of sweat pouring down his forehead in worry. Charlotte sat beside him, furtively asking the paramedics if there was anything she could do to help.

"Please be okay," Freddie whispered. Nicholas suddenly looked like a baby bird with a broken wing. His larger-than-life personality quelled from pain and his ambition on the grid momentarily halted. A sudden and surprising urge to protect the kid came over him. But there was nothing that he could do. Nothing except for being there.

"He'll be all right," Charlotte said, placing her hand on his back. "He's in capable hands now."

If Freddie could have healed him with his own hands, he would have. He felt so helpless.

The paramedics carried the kid in the stretcher out of the building, the other people giving Nicholas a round of applause as he was picked up.

From her corner of his eye, Freddie was certain he saw Nicholas grinning through the pain. Before the door shut, Nicholas confirmed it.

"Did you see me, Freddie? Did you see how fast I went?"

Clearly the painkillers were kicking in and Freddie felt himself relax ever so slightly.

Both Freddie and Charlotte accompanied Nicholas to the hospital. The two of them fiercely gripped the hand of the other in silence as Nicholas moaned in pain before the pain medication knocked him out cold.

Freddie sat beside Nicholas the whole ride to the hospital,

keeping his eyes firmly fixed on the kid. He would have done anything to trade places with him.

At the hospital, Charlotte sat beside him as Nicholas went in for scans. The two of them stood beside the examining table, holding Nicholas' good hand, as the doctor told them all that Nicholas had dislocated his left shoulder and suffering only mild surface wounds that had been disinfected. By now, Nicholas had been provided ample pain medication and had a sleepy, dazed look on his face. Freddie guessed that he would have to repeat the news to Nicholas later.

"Does that mean I have to stop racing?" were the first words out of Nicholas' mouth.

The doctor laughed. "Yes. But only for at least three months. The good news is you didn't tear anything. No muscles shredded or ligaments damaged. You're lucky. Still, you're going to need physiotherapy to get your joint nice and strong again."

Nicholas nodded and Freddie breathed a sigh of relief. "We can manage that," Freddie said.

The doctor paused, looking to each of their faces. "My grandson was on the grid today with my son-in-law. Heard that this guy here is going to be our next champion racer."

Nicholas' face burst into such a smile, which lasted for the next twenty-minutes until he fell asleep. That smile *almost* made the injury worth it.

A lot of questions pestered Freddie as he sat in that waiting room. Why had Charlotte accompanied them to the hospital so willingly? He hadn't even asked. She had stepped into that ambulance and sat by his side, clutching his hand with a look of concern on her face. Even more daunting was a question he could really ask comfortably: why had Charlotte kissed him at the race course? Of course, he didn't really care why. He really just cared that it had happened. But it opened up a lot of other questions that he still needed to ask. Why had she left ten years ago? Why hadn't she reached out? Why was she back?

He had never liked simplicity or riddles that were too easy to figure out. A challenge had always suited him just fine. It was why he tinkered with Italian cars and had relationships with complicated women. But no one was more complicated, or dazzling, than Charlotte.

The mood was gone from the kiss. Hospital waiting rooms, crying children, and dislocated shoulders tended to have that effect. He had dislocated his own shoulder once while skiing. This had been early on in his racing career. That injury had nearly ruined him—both physically and emotionally. During that time he couldn't race. He couldn't do much of anything except sit inside his own head and focus on physiotherapy. During that time, he had learned discipline. He had learned patience. But most importantly, he had learned that timing was everything. When he was finally in peak condition and ready to get back in a racecar, it was coincidentally the same day that Stiegl Laakvich retired. A spot opened up. He spent the next year hustling. After a team went through their reserve drivers, placing them in one of the twenty driving seats for F1, no one matched up. Until Freddie.

Hustling was an important part of success. Innate talent was important, but it was nothing compared to the hard work that went into something. Nicholas had the innate talent, which was saying something. It was clear he was passionate, but that was different from hard work. Hard work was what would come from the next few months of physiotherapy. *Then* they would see how much he really wanted it.

"I should get going," Charlotte said eventually from the seat beside him after an hour of waiting.

"You can't go," Freddie protested. "Who will I sit with in silence?" he teased, allowing a big grin to form on his face.

Charlotte smirked. "I think you'll be just fine. I have to check-in on my mémé. I'm making lunch for us and then I'm accompanying her to her own physiotherapy."

It struck Freddie that he hadn't asked about Charlotte's mémé to her directly, but he saw her sometimes around Monaco. She always waved at him and smiled politely, saying nothing more. Freddie had initially felt embarrassed and shy to go up to her—things had ended so strangely and it was clear that Marguerite Levant wasn't the type to reminisce. He had only heard about her fall through the grapevine. He had always liked Marguerite and had hoped she was all right.

"She's doing okay," Charlotte said, as if reading his thoughts. "She doesn't seem to really need me around. It's more the company that she likes, I suppose."

Freddie stood up to kiss her goodbye and Charlotte offered a cheek. He wasn't going to get that lucky—twice in one day. "I'll see you soon," he said, feeling certain that he would start the next race in first place.

Charlotte nodded, her smile faltering slightly as if she wasn't so sure, before turning to leave.

Freddie sat back down, knowing that he was in big trouble. He was falling in love with Charlotte all over again. He knew he *should* have felt fearful. She had broken his heart once before. But this was just like before a race. He felt nothing but adrenaline, visualizing the outcome that he wanted. Charlotte, and all of her. That tactic had served him well on the racetrack. He had no idea how it would play out in real life. Time would tell. Luckily, time had been on his side for years. "Freddie the First" was the nickname he got on his team for beating out his opponents and racing to the finish line first. No one was calling him that now. He would just have to prove it to himself.

THIRTEEN

Charlotte

"You're home! How was your morning?" Marguerite asked her as she walked in the front door.

Charlotte beamed. "Just wonderful," she said dreamily. "Well, a little not-so-wonderful too. Mémé, I have something to tell you..."

It was gnawing at her to tell her mémé the truth about where she was and whom she spent her time with. She didn't know what was worse: that her emotions had completely overcome her and she had kissed Freddie or that Nicholas had become injured. Both would inevitably be painful to recover from.

She hadn't wanted to confess that she had seen Freddie. She certainly didn't want to tell her mémé that she had been spending time with Nicholas. It was deception. It was lying. Guilt-ridden and confused, Charlotte hadn't wanted to breathe a word of her behavior. She felt ashamed.

Still, she couldn't help but feel like her shoulders were lighter. Her heart fluttered. Her thoughts were draped in a swath of breezy linen, protecting her from sadness. She was happy and guilty and she couldn't help herself.

It felt completely and utterly like love.

She knew it was time to confess. Secrets had long been her game. There was too much she was holding in and she felt ready to burst. Telling her mémé the truth as the two of them sat side by side on her mémé's sofa was the easy part.

The words spilled out of her like soup from a tipped bowl. Smooth, easy, and fluid.

"...and I think, I think I'm in love," she finished, biting down her lip. "In love with Freddie and of course I've always loved Nicholas."

She was able to breathe even more fully once the words were out. Her words hung in the air. The hard part was now. Waiting for a response. The silence as she awaited judgment or scolding. But she was just glad to have told the truth.

"I know," her mémé said, locking eyes with Charlotte and smiling.

Those two words, coupled with her mémé's tears, meant a lot more than Charlotte knew that she knew. Her mémé always knew. She didn't know how. But the two of them shed tears and didn't ask any more from each other for a few minutes. She was reunited with her son. Her son was reunited with his father. It was what she had always wanted. If only she wasn't the only one who knew... her and mémé.

"When will you tell them?" her mémé eventually asked, looking suddenly serious.

Charlotte shifted on the sofa and swallowed a lump in her throat that wouldn't seem to budge. She knew her mémé wasn't talking about telling them her feelings. The thought of telling them the truth made her head spin. "I—I don't know."

Her mémé took both of her hands in her own. "My dear, you must be very careful. You are not just dating and having fun, lighthearted and harmless. This is serious. This is Freddie and Nicholas' life. There are some things you can't be too cautious about."

Charlotte nodded, a cold sensation running through her.

"If you plan to stay in their lives," her mémé continued. "I don't think you should do it lightly. These are not people who you can have as acquaintances. If you and Freddie are anything like you were ten years ago, you will be stuck to one another like magnets. You know it, too. I think you need to tell the truth. Or..."

The 'or' was the plan that Charlotte had all along. Her original plan of finding out a little bit of information, imparting her wisdom, and leaving had failed. *She* had failed.

Charlotte sat on that couch long after her mémé had gotten up with the help of her cane, managed to the kitchen, and make them each cups of tea.

Ahead of her, Charlotte saw two roads she could drive down. That first road looked smooth at the beginning but there was inevitable rocky terrain ahead. Perhaps even a steep drop off. She could continue seeing and spending time with Freddie and Nicholas *but* with the intention to eventually tell Freddie the truth, and then he would be able to decide how to proceed with Nicholas. Nicholas was, after all, under his care. It would buy her time to continue to spend time with them. When the truth came out, it could ruin everything—their relationship, Nicholas' perception of his whole life... it could mean that everything that had been built would be shattered. Freddie would inevitably question his entire existence. Possibly, he would hate her. It could mean that their lives may be destroyed, inevitably rebuilt, but she would never know. Surely, they would insist that she no longer be apart of it. At least it would buy her some time before having to talk about that awful truth.

That second road was a quick turn. She didn't know where it led but it seemed to be going nowhere. That other option was always there, one that she had mentally prepared for, although now seemed to have lost some of its appeal—she could leave again.

Leaving quietly meant that Freddie and Nicholas could continue to build the beautiful life they seemed to be sharing and no one would get hurt. At least, there would be *less* hurt. Freddie would wonder what happened but it was recoverable. It was her original plan, and although she would be late to sticking with it, she could still stick to it.

Both seemed like terrible options.

Charlotte felt sick to her stomach making any decision. How could she have ever believed that spending one or two more visits with them was possible? In hindsight, it seemed so obvious. She should have known. She should have predicted this. How had she been so careless? So stupid? So selfish?

"You weren't selfish," her mémé said gently, placing one of her steady, cold hands over her own shaking ones. Charlotte realized she had been murmuring it aloud. "You weren't ready for that child. The Stefanos gave him a good life."

Charlotte's eyes welled to the brim. "But Freddie... he could have been ready to be a father..."

Marguerite sighed. "Yes, I've thought of this myself over the years. I don't know if the decision was the right one, from everyone's perspective, but it wasn't a bad decision. It wasn't careless. It was with Nicholas' best future in mind."

Charlotte nodded on autopilot. She had been telling herself that same script for ten years.

FOURTEEN
Freddie

Freddie stared at the glimmering diamonds from outside the store. Each one sparkled more than the next. He had never seriously looked at them before although he could easily imagine one on Charlotte's dainty finger. He hadn't stopped thinking about her. He couldn't stop thinking about her. Wracked with a million questions, but he only really cared about her answer to *one* in particular. He was going to go long. Forget laps around the track: he was ready for Le Mans.

"Is Charlotte your girlfriend?" Nicholas asked out of the blue.

Nicholas had been a champ at the hospital. All of the physicians and nurses had said so. Wearing a sling and cast, he hadn't once complained about the pain. Freddie worried about the impact it would have on his mood, since Nicholas had made such leaps since he had started racing cars. So far, he seemed okay. Truthfully, Freddie had been worried about him. He had remained calm for Nicholas' sake. But when the kid had been discharged, he had wanted to hug the life out of him he had felt so relieved. Luckily, the cast and common-sense had kept him from doing so.

He was actually coming around to having the kid around. When they had gotten home from the hospital, the two of them had watched Diehard until Nicholas fell asleep. It had sparked tenderness in him that he hadn't previously known.

"She was my girlfriend at one point," Freddie began to explain, tearing his eyes from the rings and turning to Nicholas, who peered up at him with wide eyes.

"What happened?"

Freddie laughed uncertainly. "That's a great question. Only she knows. But to put it simply, I guess she left. Got spooked by my dad, who thought a relationship would throw a wrench into my career."

"So she left because she didn't want to get in the way of your racing success?" Nicholas echoed.

"Yeah, sounds pretty dumb when you put it that way," Freddie laughed. "But we were young and dumb. Kids."

"I'm a kid," Nicholas said.

"Yes, but you're not dumb," Freddie countered.

"So your dad made her leave? What happened? Where's your dad now?"

Nicholas frowned. He didn't talk much about his parents. Never had he spoken about them candidly, especially so openly. They were out on a public street. Anyone could hear them and he didn't want to redline it. Besides, he didn't know how much truth was appropriate to disclose to Nicholas. He decided to give the condensed version. When Nicholas was older, he could tell him the whole story.

"He's in Kentucky. That's in the USA."

Nicholas rolled his eyes. "I know where Kentucky is. Do you visit him?"

"Rarely."

"How come? Does he visit you?"

"Not really. Hey, did you want to grab a gelato?" Freddie asked with forced enthusiasm. Anything to hopefully change the topic.

"Let's stay on track," Nicholas said seriously. "It sounds like you don't have much of a relationship with your dad anymore."

Freddie sighed. "Look, it's complicated. More complicated than I wish to discuss today. But one day I'll tell you the full story, okay?"

Nicholas nodded, seemingly appeased. "I think that you would have liked my dad," he said quietly. "I know he would have loved you."

Freddie felt momentarily paralyzed by emotion, warmth in his chest that made it difficult to take a full breath. "I know your dad certainly loved you."

"Do you love me?" Nicholas asked, his words innocent and his eyes searching for hope.

Oh boy. Freddie knew that there were certain moments in life that couldn't be taken back. Certain moments that determined an entire friendship, relationship, family tie. It was imperative to see these moments, guard them, and do whatever it took to protect them. He only had one chance to win with this kind of question.

"Yes?" he answered sincerely yet anxiously. Was that the right answer? He knew that he was being truthful. Still, it felt overwhelming to discuss. He waited for Nicholas' response in active suspension.

Nicholas smiled, looking pleased at the response. "I love Miranda."

Freddie balked, feeling like he had been sucker-punched. "*Miranda*?"

Nodding, Nicholas looked very serious. "She's a girl in my class. The most beautiful girl in the world."

Freddie vaguely recalled Nicholas having mentioned Miranda, back when they had taken Charlotte out for that first date. He remembered Charlotte looking so attentive as Nicholas spoke. He, of course, had been enraptured in Charlotte's melodic laughter. He hadn't been paying much attention to what Nicholas was saying that day. Struggling to remember the exact details, he nodded, hoping he pulled off a convincing act.

"Right, Miranda. So, she's your... *girlfriend*?"

Nicholas scoffed. "I wish. She is so cool. But she doesn't even know I exist."

"So how do you get her attention?" Freddie wondered aloud.

"I was thinking the accordion is a unique instrument..."

Freddie frowned. "The accordion? Do you play?"

Nicholas shook his head. "Not yet…"

"You've got it, kid. You've got it. The talent, the skill..."

"So you think I should get an accordion?" Nicholas asked hopefully.

"No, no, no. Definitely not that. *Anything* but that," Freddie said quickly. He couldn't imagine anything worse to improve the kid's prospects with Miranda… and he couldn't imagine Sundays being dedicated to accordion practice. "No, you're a racer. You drive faster than anyone I've seen in a long time. Well, for people starting out that is. And you're brave. You're not going to let this injury stand in your way, are you champ?"

Nicholas slowly shook his head side to side. "No way. I'm getting back in that car," he said determinedly.

"That's my boy!"

Becoming a full-time caregiver to a nine-year old was harder work than Freddie had imagined. It was constantly inspecting for damage. All of a sudden, his sleek bachelor pad was... *different.* The surfaces, once minimalist and empty, were now covered in comic books. The walls, once bare except for the few black and white photographs of him racing, had posters of *other* racecar drivers and racecars that had been thumbtacked to the walls. Freddie saw the posters tacked up in what was previously his office, now Nicholas' room, and shut the door. No use in arguing, no point trying to fight it. At least Nicholas was passionate about the same stuff as him.

And contrary to his reaction a few weeks earlier, he actually didn't mind the clutter. The no longer flinched when he saw the thumbtacks hanging pictures on the walls in Nicholas' room—even if they were of other drivers and teams than the ones he had driven on. He had even stopped calling it the guest bedroom and it was now Nicholas' room.

Although Freddie had offered to let Nicholas stay home sick due to his injury, the kid had persisted. It was baffling to Freddie, who had never enjoyed school a day in his life. Except, of course, those classes with Charlotte. But when Nicholas was at school, Freddie's day passed rather slowly. He didn't have the hustle and bustle of jetting to new cities anymore. There was nothing for him to train for. He had saved his money very well over his racing career. So long as he remained on budget, he wouldn't have to work a day more in his life. Taking on Nicholas as a full-time guardian also meant that there was an additional influx of cash from the Stefano Estate. They had set aside a trust for Nicholas and his caregiver, in the event of an untimely death. Plus, Nicholas would have an even bigger trust fund allotted to him when he turned eighteen. Since money wasn't an issue, his day-to-day activities really depended on his motivations and desires alone. The problem was, he only wanted to see one person. And she wasn't answering his texts.

It was strange how seeing Charlotte again felt so easy yet drastically different. Being in her company was the easiest thing in the world. In fact, being with her made life feel even *easier*. At the same time, her presence made him realize the gaping hole in his life—the emptiness and longing he had for that kind of connection. Charlotte and him went together like the sea and sand. Complimentary yet different, they existed peacefully together. He felt with conviction that it was time to be bold. Goodbye to the slow-moving, cautious Freddie who had patiently waited for Charlotte for ten years. He was ready to introduce her to the new Freddie—life in the fast lane.

He had a feeling she would like it.

In his pocket, he was carrying a small wooden ring-box, which carried a yellow gold engagement ring with three one-carat diamonds lined up side-by-side. One diamond for him, one diamond for her, and one diamond for Nicholas. It was odd, sure. But he was now the legal guardian of this kid. Any woman who came into his life would have to accept that he was a package deal. For some reason, he thought that Charlotte wouldn't mind it one bit. In fact, she had taken to Nicholas the way he had taken to racing, and Nicholas to her. He hoped that managing Nicholas that evening would be like going on cruise control.

His heart pounding through his chest, Freddie would ask Nicholas later what he thought about two things: his opinion on asking

Charlotte to marry him and what he thought of the ring. He had his fingers crossed that Nicholas would give a big thumbs up for each.

He knew it was swift. He knew that a lot had changed. But why not be bold? Why not go after what he really wanted in life? Sure, things hadn't exactly worked out the way that he had planned. His life hadn't always been always gone the way he dreamed. But he had worked hard. He had accomplished amazing things. He was going to go after what he really wanted, which he realized now was a happy family. Growing up, that was the furthest thing from his experience. Now, that family was being cobbled together in the most unexpected of ways, but surely he could make it work. There were no airbags in this situation. If it went well, he would win. But if it didn't... he certainly didn't want to crash and burn. Still, it was a risk he was willing to take.

Spending the afternoon daydreaming about Charlotte and asking her to be his wife, the daily chores of prepping dinner for him and Nicholas, cleaning the kitchen, and going grocery shopping flew by. He barely recognized himself but he actually liked this new routine. This new idea of who he could be. For the last ten years, he had thought his life would look totally different from how it turned out. *Why not embrace it?* When Freddie drove to pick up Nicholas from school, he felt immediately pulled to the present moment upon seeing Nicholas' expression.

Glee. Pure and total joy. From ear to ear, Nicholas was brimming with happiness. It was enough to make all of Freddie's anxiety about asking Charlotte to marry him disappear.

"Good day at school?" Freddie ventured, as Nicholas buckled himself into his seat.

Nicholas turned to him, barely able to contain his excitement. "There's a talent contest," the kid said before even saying hello.

Freddie nodded, trying to hide his feelings of confusion. "Right, that's great!" he said with enthusiasm.

"I'm going to race and show Miranda how amazing I am," Nicholas declared.

Suddenly it clicked. "Right, Miranda. So, did you talk to her today?"

Nicholas shook his head but didn't look defeated. "No, but I got her to look at me. Everyone was signing my cast. When I told people how I got it, everyone seemed really excited."

"I'll bet," Freddie laughed. He remembered how kids could be. Back when he had started racing, he had mentioned it to one of his classmates. Before he knew it, almost half the class had signed up for lessons. Within a month, the throng had thinned as his classmates enjoyed the first lap but didn't like it enough to continue regularly. There were other more social and less demanding sports that they enjoyed more. Others had loved the race but hated losing, and that hatred of losing made them quit. For the select few, they had loved racing and hated losing, but that hatred of losing had instead made them work harder to *win.* Those people were few and far between. Then there were the very few, like Nicholas and Freddie way back in the day. They had natural talent, loved the game, and hated losing so much that they would do *anything* to win. In Nicholas' case, it had resulted in a dislocated shoulder. Freddie knew that if Nicholas were to continue, he would have to teach the kid how to race safely so that he didn't stack one injury atop of another.

Nicholas continued talking as Freddie slowly pulled out of the school's pick-up and drop-off zone. He was stalled in a line of Mercedes, Porches, and BMWs when from out of the corner of his eye he saw a woman was frantically waving to him from the grass. Freddie pulled to a stop, thinking it must be one of Nicholas' teachers. As the woman got closer, Freddie wished he could disappear into the Monaco streets in a flash. But this was a school zone, and it would be rude.

"Hi strangers!" came Violet's exuberant voice. "Nice to see you, Freddie. What are you doing here?"

"I should ask the same," Freddie replied coolly. Violet had been his blind spot. He hadn't known when they were together how much he had put himself in danger by being around her. He still treaded with caution.

Violet looked delighted to respond as she flipped her hair. "Well, now that you asked, my boyfriend asked me to pick up his son. You remember? I told you at the racetrack?"

Freddie nodded while keeping his eyes straight ahead. "Right, well—"

"—I shouldn't ask, it's none of my business, but Nicholas, you were the Stefanos son?"

Before Freddie could reply or drive away, Nicholas piped up. "I still am. Always will be."

Violet laughed as if Nicholas had just made the funniest joke she had ever heard. "Right, right, of course. My mistake. So why are you all of a sudden his guardian, Freddie?"

Freddie took the car out of park and began inching forward. She had a way of prodding that was about as fun as brake pads failing.

"Nice catching up with you," he called out the window, more for appearances sake. He didn't want to set a bad example for Nicholas. He shook his head and muttered something under his breath that he *didn't* want to set an example for Nicholas. Not so much as a 'hello' to Nicholas or asking about his arm, which she had plainly witnessed. How had he been so blind before?

"That woman gets under my skin," Freddie said to Nicholas once they were in the clear. "I'm sorry about that. She's an ex-girlfriend. A nosy ex-girlfriend. She thinks she's still entitled to know my business. *Our* business."

Nicholas frowned. "How could you date someone like that? Knowing that there are Charlotte's in the world?"

Freddie laughed, because this time Nicholas had said the funniest thing in the world, at least to him. "I don't know, kid. But with you looking out for me, I can guarantee you I won't make that mistake again."

FIFTEEN

Violet

Violet sipped a glass of champagne from the yacht deck. Her fiancé's new boat was exactly to her liking and she had outfitted it to her own taste and specifications. Her husband-to-be, Yanic, was sweet. He was patient and gentle and kind. He was nothing like her and she knew it. The only person who seemed totally unaware of their differences was Yanic.

All was fair when it came to love and war. That's what her own mother had taught her. And in order to take care of yourself, you had to put yourself first. Every. Single. Time. She had lived at both the depths of poverty and the highest bracket of wealth. She had worked hard to get to where she was, and although she knew what people thought of her, she had put in methodical work to get there. It wasn't a free ride.

"I'll have another," she called to one of the staff members aboard the yacht. "Thank you, Tabitha," she said as she saw who approached. "Will you join me?"

Tabitha, a middle-aged woman who had a joyful laugh and deep tan, shook her head. "I'm afraid not, *madame*. My contract prohibits the use of alcohol on board the ship while I'm on duty."

Violet nodded her head understandingly. "Right," she said

quickly. "No problem. Just one glass of champagne then."

Loneliness was a vicious emotion. Even with everything she had ever dreamt of right at her fingertips, that silly, stupid emotion could come up at any point. Even when she had surrounded herself with throngs of people at parties. She needed gasoline but the only thing available was diesel. She was stuck.

She sipped her champagne quietly, enjoying the sounds that the seagulls made as they swooped down and cawed out to the abyss beyond the horizon line.

Freddie was definitely up to something. And that kid certainly had some sort of a story attached. Her mind was reeling, trying to come up with some plausible explanation. Of course, Charlotte returning to Monaco so suddenly certainly added a fascinating layer to it all. How could she weave all of that together?

Randolph didn't care if her story was real or not. He just cared that it sold well beyond his buying price. What kind of a story could she swing from this?

"*Madame*, would you like to speak with Yanic and Pierre?" Tabitha asked, pointing towards the deck phone. "They are about to meet with Justine."

Justine was Yanic's ex-wife and Pierre's mother. Pierre was going to Justine's before Yanic's bachelor party and her own bachelorette. Yanic and Justine had an amicable divorce and Pierre split his time between both parents. It was unlike anything she had ever seen before. Truthfully, the idea of being a stepmother was about as far from her mind as the truth regarding the story she was going to sell about Freddie.

Something clicked in Violet's mind. "No, no thank you," she said quickly, grabbing her phone to text herself the details of her whirlwind concoction. Her mind whirred like a V8 engine. "His son…" she muttered.

The entire world drowned out as she typed, feeling more and more certain that this was the story that needed to go to press. The truth? That was for amateurs. She had dabbled in the truth before and look how it had hurt Freddie? Sure, she was upset that he had ended things with her. And yes, she seemed to be a little wrapped up in the past. But she didn't want to ruin his life. Besides, this story was so crazy, so ridiculous, that she would surely make a small fortune from Randolph *and* ensure that no one was hurt in the process.

Because if the story *wasn't* true, then Freddie certainly couldn't be bothered, right?

That's what she kept telling herself over and over again. But she just needed to be certain that it wasn't true. She needed to be totally and positively certain before sending it to Randolph. She didn't mind sending off an obvious lie given that it wouldn't hurt anyone. But she needed to be certain.

It was the day before her bachelorette party. She knew exactly how she wanted to spend it. It certainly wasn't conventional, but then again, neither was she.

SIXTEEN

Charlotte

Strolling the streets of Monaco, Charlotte took everything in—the sights, the sounds, the smells, and the taste. She had needed a break from mulling over decision about what to do with Freddie and Nicholas. She bit down on a fresh croissant as she walked along a manicured street. Although most Monegasque and French never ate on the go, it was a habit she had picked up in New York City. She wouldn't be in Monaco much longer anyway, after having decided that her presence was too disruptive to the lives of Nicholas and Freddie alike. There was no way for her to remain in Monaco without the truth coming out.

The two of them seemed to be doing so well. They were reunited. They were thriving. It was all she could have ever wanted. A part of her didn't want to ruin it all with the truth. Another part wondered how much they were truly living without it.

Charlotte looked immaculate in a linen off-shoulder blouse that fitted her snugly, paired with matching capris and leather sandals. But inside, she couldn't have felt any more different. As she walked by the Oceanographic Museum, a familiar face popped up and greeted her.

"Well, if it isn't Charlotte Levant," Violet said with such excitement that Charlotte knew it had to be put on. "Out for a stroll?

Not spending the day with your boys?"

Charlotte smiled tightly. A woman who relished privacy, Violet seemed to be everywhere and liked asking lots of questions. "Just enjoying the sun," Charlotte said demurely. "Nice to see you—"

"—Just hold on there a minute," Violet continued, taking a step towards her. "How long have you and Freddie been back together? You can confide in me. I'm just curious."

Charlotte took a step backwards. She liked having her bumpers on in conversations. Violet liked to ram and hit hard. Today, she was going to have to steer things in a new direction.

"If you're after him, don't worry. I'm not standing in your way," she said curtly. "Besides, I prefer not to discuss my personal matters." Her words were only partially true. If Violet went after Freddie, she didn't truly know how she would respond.

Violet's eyes flashed. "How long ago was it that you left Monaco, Charlotte? Was it nine years or ten?"

Saying nothing, Charlotte took a deep breath. Was Violet implying what she thought?

Violet continued. "Funny how alike Freddie and Nicholas look, isn't it? Just like father and son. And boy oh boy, does Nicholas ever have Freddie's racing skills. Perhaps a natural talent?"

Violet eyed Charlotte, a knowing look in her eyes.

"Excuse me?" Charlotte sputtered.

"You heard me," Violet retorted. Slowly, the woman nodded at her, a slow and mean grin forming on her unnaturally taught face.

A fire was burning inside of Charlotte. This couldn't be happening.

As quickly as the veil had been lifted, it descended. Violet giggled and smiled sweetly. "Oh don't worry. It's our little secret," she said.

"I'm not sure what you're talking about," Charlotte managed through gritted teeth.

"My mistake."

Did Violet know? Surely she couldn't. There was no way.

Charlotte's eyes narrowed as she examined Violet, almost daring her to come out and say it. But Violet smirked and gave a little shrug.

"Well, *lovely* seeing you, as always. We must catch up soon," she drawled.

Charlotte was left on the pavement, mouth agape, wondering what had just happened. In a span of seconds, any lasting conception of allowing Freddie and Nicholas to live as they were was vanishing in a cloud of Chanel perfume. There was a gnawing feeling in her chest as she took one labored breath after another. Something she couldn't quite place. All cylinders were firing but she felt like she was going nowhere.

Could Violet know?

No. There was no way. She clearly just liked mind games.

But what if she did...

Charlotte took a deep breath. She couldn't handle her current dilemma as well as Freddie's clearly psychopathic ex. The woman was *nuts.* If she knew it, clearly Freddie did. She would just have to brush it off. *It's nothing*, she told herself. *You're being paranoid.* Besides, she had bigger things to focus on right now. She was in Monaco and trying to remember her way to the market. It was strange how quickly one could forget—especially when actively trying not to think about the city for a whole decade. There was no time to focus on Violet. A tantalizing smell wafted out from a nearby bakery and she smiled. With a dozen macarons calling her name, who could remember the half-hearted words of a jealous girl from her past?

Not Charlotte, that's who.

SEVENTEEN

Freddie

The ring sparkled in the sunlight, casting millions of light fragments on the wall as Freddie and Nicholas examined it together. The two of them had sat in silence, examining it seriously for the last ten minutes. By now, all of Freddie's worry had dissipated. Diamonds in the sun seemed to have a meditative effect.

"She can't say no," Nicholas said, a smile forming on his face. "It's too pretty."

Freddie laughed. "I think she'll like it."

His head and heart inflating like a balloon; he imagined what it would be like for them to live together. One happy family. It would be a little unconventional, sure. But Nicholas seemed happy with the idea, and he knew that he would be thrilled. Now the big question was: did Charlotte want that too?

Who was he kidding? *Of course she did.*

Freddie had transformed over the past few weeks. A cynic and skeptic about things working out, he now found himself imagining the best-case scenarios. He wasn't just imagining them: he expected it to work out.

It was all happening rather quickly, but Freddie figured he was making up for lost time. Charlotte still hadn't answered his text messages but he figured that she had left her phone at home. That evening, he would surprise her with a romantic dinner by the seaside—as originally intended, a pop the question.

Sure, it was hasty.

Yes, it was bold.

But Freddie relished those two qualities. He had been described as fast and bold on the track. He loved being in the driver's seat of his life. Wasn't life just a mirror of the racetrack? No matter how cautious and careful you were, accidents could still happen. It was no guarantee of a podium finish. Glory and winning only happened when Freddie drove like a madman, unafraid of the consequences, with only one outcome in sight. The possibility that Charlotte might say anything other than "yes" wasn't on Freddie's radar. It couldn't be. In order to get to that finish line, he could only focus on one outcome: success.

Giving Charlotte a call once again, he finally got through to her. "Meet me outside the Monte-Carlo Casino this evening. How about seven thirty?"

Charlotte agreed. She sounded tense. He was sure that she was worried about her grandmother, with whom she had always been close. She would have so much to celebrate that evening. They both would. Freddie couldn't wait.

The Monte-Carlo Casino was the perfect meeting spot. Although citizens of Monaco technically weren't allowed inside the Casino, an attempt to thwart the risk of residents losing their money gambling, it was a stunning backdrop that was all about risk. He was taking a chance. He knew that he was lucky. This wasn't just chance, it was fate. Who said that there was only first place on the podium? That evening, there would be two people standing up there sharing the trophy.

EIGHTEEN

Charlotte

After running into Violet, Charlotte had cemented her decision—she would *keep* the secret. How could Freddie and Nicholas ever manage to lead a normal life with that kind of bomb being dropped? There would be people like Violet swarming them. The paparazzi would have a field day. Freddie had always hated scandal and boy, was this ever scandalous. There was no easy decision, but after running into Violet, there was no way she could sign the two of them up for a lifetime of *those* sorts of conversations.

Charlotte took one panicked breath after another. This was it. This was going to be her goodbye to Freddie. It would be easier without Nicholas there. This was already so much more complicated than she could have ever wanted. A clean and easy break. That would be the best thing for everyone.

Now, she had a few hours before the dreaded dinner. She would tell Freddie she was leaving this time, rather than just vanishing into thin air. Something told her that if she did just leave, this time he would try to find her. He had more money and more invested this time around.

When that evening rolled around, at seven thirty on the dot, Charlotte was waiting outside of the Monte-Carlo Casino. It was a glamorous and impressive meeting spot, even if she had been there a million times before. The palm trees outside swayed in the breeze. She loved everything about the Monte Carlo neighborhood. The opulence of the building, the sense of grandness, the glittering flashes of cameras and steady stream of gamblers, tourists, and onlookers always made her smile. Monaco. She would miss this.

The green hills peaked out behind the buildings in the distance as she looked around for Freddie. A parade of super cars drove past her, parking in front of the casino in designated spots. Almost immediately, more tourists arrived with their camera, snapping pictures. Charlotte had her camera too but she resisted taking any photos. She didn't want to come across as a tourist in her own home. She already felt like she had put up walls between herself and that country. She didn't need more.

Taking it all in, she almost missed Freddie, who was standing by the perimeter of the nearby fountain, his eyes shining. As their eyes met, Charlotte's stomach flip-flopped. He looked at the picture of a dapper gentleman in his pale linen suit and light blue oxford shirt. This was going to be harder than she thought.

"Aren't you a stunner," Freddie said, leaning towards her and grazing her cheek with his lips. He smelled of soap and aftershave, and the warmth of his body pressing against her made her yearn to abort the plan entirely.

Instead, Charlotte smiled demurely. This was the last time that Freddie would see her. She had wanted to at least look presentable. With oversized Tahitian pearls and a black fitted dress that flared at the sleeves and hugged her body everywhere else, she felt pretty good about her outfit choice, but that was about the only thing she felt good about. Memories of the last time seeing someone hung around like a ghost. She wanted to make sure that her ghost represented the very best she had to offer.

"You don't look so bad yourself," she heard herself saying, immediately cursing herself for doing so. She wasn't supposed to flirt with the man she was leaving. The way Freddie was looking at her gave her butterflies. This was going to be way harder than she thought.

"Ready?" he asked, holding out his hand to hers.

This would be their last date together. Instead of feeling heartbroken, Charlotte was trying to soak up every minute of it. Every glittering moment with him. If she thought too hard about it, she would burst into tears. Instead, she focused so hard on the present moment that would have given her yoga instructor back in Manhattan a run for his money. These were their last precious moments together; she might as well enjoy it before it was all over. Taking his hand in hers, Charlotte did her best to smile.

"Ready as I'll ever be."

Dinner was magnificent. With a seaside table and candles illuminating the two of them, soft jazz music in the air from a live musician, and a decadent array of all Charlotte's favorite foods one after another, it had everything possible to be a *perfect* night. She had laughed harder, smiled bigger, and the food tasted more delicious than anything she had ever eaten before. In a way, it felt to Charlotte like her last dinner. She had tried to be present for every moment of it. Perhaps that was part of the problem. Charlotte was having such a good time; the idea of leaving this world behind again seemed too much.

If it hadn't been for the gnawing sensation growing inside her, she may have been able to distract herself from those worried thoughts. Even Freddie seemed a bit on edge with his fidgety hands and darting eyes making him look more nervous than she had ever seen him. Of course, neither of them said a thing about it, each doing their best to play it cool.

The restaurant Freddie had chosen was stunning. *La Sirena* was clearly a hotspot, with a line snaking out the front. The maître d' said the same thing to everyone: without a reservation, you're not getting in. A recent third Michelin-star made *La Sirena* an undeniable success and celebrity sightings meant that all the tourists were now flocking. Freddie and Charlotte had one of the ten coveted tables—arguably the best, most private one. The restaurant, all beige concrete and smooth marble, looked straight out of an architectural magazine. The waves nearly crashed onto the deck where their table was set up. If it weren't for the glass barrier, Charlotte was sure the turbulent, wild water would have soaked her from head to toe.

Freddie smiled at her from across the table. They had discussed everything from racing to Monaco to how Charlotte's grandmother was doing, steering clear of any hot button topics—namely Nicholas, New York, or their past. It was like no time had passed at all. They had laughed until tears streamed down her face. She had forgotten how funny he was. They spoke about serious things, like Freddie's retirement from racing. He asked her about New York and her job, which she spoke about with reverence. New York City and her life there felt a million miles away and a million lifetimes ago. Freddie cleared his throat.

"I have something to ask you..."

Charlotte took a deep breath, bracing herself for a tough question. "Yes?"

"Why did you leave Monaco? Ten years, I've been wondering."

Charlotte's pulse quickened. "Look, it's complicated," she managed, her voice shaking. She reached for her glass of water with a trembling hand.

"Right, right, of course. I don't mean to pry," Freddie nodded, as if she had just said something profound. "Was it my father?" he added quickly.

Charlotte's mind went in every possible direction. She remembered that conversation with Stewart Ridgeport like it had been yesterday. On the couch, after Freddie had just gotten up to grab them more water, Stewart came up to her and told her that Freddie didn't need distractions—not her, not a baby, *nothing*. Freddie's father hadn't known that she was pregnant, but the fact that her and Freddie were all over one another had clearly been a tip off. Those words had sent a chill down her spine, haunting her for days and nights as she cradled her still-flat belly. She couldn't blame Stewart for her decision to give up Nicholas, but his words certainly had provided a bit of a push.

How was she supposed to answer Freddie's question? She was

panicking. "Look," she began, licking her suddenly parched lips. "I can explain..."

"Would the *madame* care for a refill?"

Charlotte had never felt so grateful or glad to see a waiter in her entire life. Nodding gratefully, she held up her half-full wine glass and allowed it to be topped up. She glugged down almost as much as the waiter had poured as soon as he left.

"Well," Charlotte fumbled. "You see—"

Waving his hands frantically, Freddie stopped her. "Charlotte, I've made you uncomfortable. That's the last thing I wanted for this evening. Forgive me?"

Nodding slowly, not fully sure what was happening, Freddie stooped onto one knee. For a moment, Charlotte assumed he had dropped something and thought nothing of it. Only when he cupped her hands in his and he stared into her eyes, as if staring into her soul, did Charlotte clue in. She leapt from the seat as if it were on fire.

"No, no, no, no, no," Charlotte muttered, her heart racing and adrenaline coursing through body.

Freddie seemed to be on a planet of his own, ostensibly oblivious to Charlotte's state. "Charlotte," he began, his voice quivering and his face the picture of someone who only envisioned success ahead of him. "Charlotte Levant..."

Everything was moving in slow motion—from the way that Freddie looked up at her with hope, to the way he opened that tiny box, revealing a perfect ring with three diamonds. Her vision blurred around the edges, like headlights through a thick fog. Everyone was turning in their seats to look at them. She could feel the weight of their attention on her, on the ring, on *them*. It was as if Charlotte was in the middle of a dream where she wanted to move but her feet were planted to the ground, stuck, heavy and unmoving. This felt stranger than a dream. This felt like it was happening to someone else.

Those four words brought the reality crashing back to the present moment.

"...will you marry me?"

NINETEEN

Charlotte

There are four words that could change life forever. In Charlotte's case, it wasn't a change for the good. In fact, those words were arguably the worst thing she could have heard. At least at that specific moment in time.

They were words Charlotte had dreamt about. Hearing them aloud was as magnificent as she had ever dreamt. But it was the cavalcade of reminders of the truth that made everything feel like her entire world and everything that she loved was crashing down in front of her.

Neat and tidy, clean lines, boundaries. That was how Charlotte liked to live her life. Those boundaries had protected her for the last decade. A shell that she needed. But she had ignored the check engine light that had popped into her mind so many times since she started to spend time with Freddie and Nicholas, choosing to ignore it and continue to drive at a reckless speed. It was inevitable that it would all break down. She had been foolish and allowed herself to fall prey to her own desires. All those boundaries she had let down since meeting Nicholas... she knew she never should have allowed things to go as far as they had with Freddie and she should have never allowed Nicholas to get close to her.

But Charlotte didn't like to dwell. She didn't like thinking back to hard times and when she did, she fought it tooth and nail. It had always been in the back of her mind that coming back to Monaco could ruin everything she had worked to rebuild over the last ten years. It was all so close to falling apart. Just as she thought she would be able to draw a line in the sand and tell Freddie she was leaving, he went ahead and said those words.

Those four silly words. Those four wonderful words.

After Freddie had proposed, Charlotte had fled the restaurant as fast as her legs would carry her. She hadn't said anything—not yes, not no. She felt a coward and hated herself for it. But she was doing him a favor in the long run. She was going to ruin his life if she stayed. She would ruin Nicholas' life. *That is, if she hadn't already,* she thought ominously.

That stupid, darn secret. Every part of her wished that she had done something differently—both ten years ago and ten minutes earlier. Every part of her wished she had done things differently back then.

Every part of her had wanted to say *yes*.

True to her old reputation, Charlotte was unwavering, even to herself. This could have been a chance for real change. In hindsight, of course there was always the option to have said yes. But at the time, there had only been one answer: run away. There was the ring, gorgeous and sparkling. Three diamonds. They could have been dirty rocks—it wouldn't have mattered. What mattered was the fragile, beaming face staring back at her.

Leaving would inevitably break Freddie's heart but at least it would spare Nicholas. Surely, he would just be confused and probably think of her as an adult as a strange and funny chapter in his adopted dad's life. It would spare him the heartache of the truth, which would have to come out if she had stayed. Besides, staying and saying 'yes' was no guarantee that it would be 'happily-ever-after'. Wasn't there just as big of a chance that they didn't end up a family because they wouldn't want her in their lives *and* they had to live with the secret?

No, much better just to be the awful person who left and cleanly broke Freddie's heart. Nicholas was young. He could recover.

As she lay on her childhood bed, she imagined the possibility that she *could* have stayed, done the hardest thing in the world and told him the truth, and see if he still wanted to give things a shot. Her vocal chords retracted just thinking about saying those words.

Some moments, she felt she had blown it. Her one chance. But mostly since the proposal, she felt a gnawing sensation in her stomach. Even a bit of relief. Her time for being curious was *done*. She could rest easy. *Freddie would ultimately be okay—he would recover from this.* And Nicholas would surely be shaken by this, but he was ultimately doing well. In fact, he seemed to be doing great.

It had always been a big question mark—how would this end? At least now she knew. If she got any closer, she would feel compelled to tell them the truth or leave without any reason. Freddie's proposal had simplified things in some ways. It had sped up the inevitable.

The one silver lining was now Freddie would never wonder why she had left. He would presumably chalk her behavior up to her fear of commitment or whatever it was he already thought of her. At least she hadn't had to tell him outright that she was leaving. That conversation was one she had dreaded more than anything.

Charlotte was so wrapped up in her thoughts as she packed her bags, so disconnected from her feelings to protect herself, that she barely noticed her mémé as she entered her bedroom.

"So, you're leaving Monaco?" her mémé asked, giving away nothing with her tone.

Charlotte exhaled and met her mémé's eye line. This whole experiment of coming back to Monaco had been a lemon. "What choice do I have?"

Her mémé cocked her head to the side and shrugged, as if they were deciding what to order for dinner and not whether she should leave Monaco forever and keep her secret, or if she should stay and tell the truth, possibly rupturing Nicholas and Freddie's life forever. "Are you at least going to listen to what the boy has to say?"

"He already said everything he needed to say," Charlotte muttered. She was a coward. A fool. She also felt a moral duty to protect her son. *Wasn't this the best way?*

She wished that she didn't have to repeat what had happened to anyone, but somehow talking with her mémé, the words came tumbling out despite her misgivings. She took a deep breath before allowing her to say the dreaded thing that caused her tremendous pain and joy. "He asked me to marry him."

"Do you love him?" her mémé asked seriously.

Charlotte flushed. *Love* was the very last thing on her mind. She didn't exactly feel in a position to trust her heart either. It had already gotten her into this situation, and the one ten years before. So far, listening to her heart didn't seem to be doing her many favors.

"That doesn't matter," she replied meekly. Her throat suddenly felt all tight and scratchy as heat rose to her cheeks.

"I know you love Nicholas. That much is obvious," her mémé said. "I worry that leaving *again* isn't going to solve your problems quite like you hope."

"By leaving, I'm protecting them. I saw what I needed to see—the two of them are okay. They'll be shaken up by this, but hopefully they can laugh about it in years to come. I'm protecting them."

"Are you sure it's them you're protecting?"

Charlotte buried her head in her hands.

Her mémé's eyebrows shot up. "My darling girl, look at me."

Charlotte forced herself to look up at her mémé, whose kind eyes made her feel just the tiniest bit better.

"You've been running for a long time," her mémé continued. "Now, we tried our best that first time around ten years ago. Were some mistakes made? Of course. No one is perfect. But I did my best, you did your best, and the Stefanos did their best. Didn't Freddie turn out to become a wonderful Formula One driver, just like you had wanted? And didn't Nicholas have a stable, happy upbringing with two extremely loving and adoring parents?"

Her head was spinning. "I suppose..."

Her mémé clucked her tongue. "Charlotte, you made a mistake. I made a mistake, advising you as I did. Don't think that I don't think about it everyday, because I do. Freddie should have known. We know that now. But back then, things were different. You were different, he was different, I was different, the whole situation was different—"

"—I get it," Charlotte said. "Things were different."

"Exactly. Now, are you going to punish yourself forever? Are you going to deprive yourself of knowing your son for the rest of your entire life because of this? Perhaps you're right. Maybe the truth ruins the relationship you have with them. But you're his mother. Don't you think there's a chance he may want to rebuild that relationship with you? Even if it looks different?"

Charlotte sat in silence, trying to think of a suitable response. Truthfully, she didn't know. "You think I'm trying to protect myself, not them, don't you?"

Her mémé evaded the question. "Aren't you tired of hiding this secret? Remember Charlotte, what is brought into the light can no longer be dark."

Charlotte looked up, her eyes welling with tears. The ramifications of a secret like that couldn't just be undone with the truth.

Her stubborn streak kicked in. "I know how this will play out if I stay," said, restating what she had been mulling over since she left the restaurant. "If I take a gamble and decide to forgive myself, to allow myself a chance at happiness, and accept the marriage proposal, inevitably telling the truth to Freddie, I'll ruin everything. Everyone will get hurt, possibly beyond repair. Including Nicholas. *Especially* Nicholas. Things with Freddie and Nicholas are going well. It's such a delicate situation already, I can't risk their happiness just for a lighter conscience."

"Maybe you don't accept the marriage proposal. Maybe you just tell the truth."

"Everyone will get hurt."

"Everyone is already hurt." Her mémé took Charlotte's hands

in hers. "It's true that the truth might hurt. But don't you think that healing comes after the hurt? The hurt will be there, but it opens up that door for a whole new chapter. After all, you don't learn to drive in one day. Let alone a vehicle as sensitive and finely tuned as Freddie Ridgeport. That takes time and patience, my dear."

Charlotte didn't say anything, allowing the words to wash over her charred ego instead. She picked at her cuticles.

"I'm going to try to tell you this another way that might make more sense," her mémé continued. "To use my favorite metaphor, you have a garden. A beautiful garden. It's grown glorious in recent years. But coming back to Monaco, your garden is being uprooted and dirt is being flung everywhere in the process. Of course, that makes you wildly uncomfortable. You hate mess, Charlotte. But after all that uprooting, you see the root rot in those beautiful plants. They might look nice, but they're not healthy. The planters they're in? They also needed new foundations. They had gotten cracked over the years."

Charlotte took a deep breath. As she exhaled, her whole body shuddered. "So what you're saying is my life is like a broken planter?"

"No, I'm saying *you* are the broken planter," her mémé with a hearty laugh. "This is the time to heal yourself. You might be able to sprout daisies somewhere else, but they're going to keep dying unless you come back to the root of the problem."

Charlotte felt momentarily stung by her mémé's words, no matter how jovially they had been delivered. Still, she knew that they came from a place of love. Most importantly, she knew that what her mémé had said hurt because it was true.

"So," she began, kicking one bare foot against the other. "How do I fix my foundation or whatever it was you called it?" Charlotte asked.

Her mémé smiled warmly and patted her hand. "That, *mon cherie*, is up to you to figure out."

In silence, her mémé stood up and gave an almost imperceptible wink before striding out. It dawned on Charlotte that her mémé was no longer using a cane to get around. When had that happened? She had come to Monaco to help her grandmother, yet all she had managed to do was get more tightly wound and wrapped up in her own mess. Perhaps her mémé was right. Perhaps her foundation was cracked. How on Earth could she fix it and could it happen in a few hours?

Charlotte stopped packing her belongings and sat in her old bedroom. Staring at her old childhood relics, her eyes stopped on an item that she hadn't seen in a decade. She had been staying in this room for weeks and it was like she was seeing her desk anew. On top of the antique dresser was a small wooden box which Charlotte already knew held a treasure dear to her heart. Carefully, she opened up the box and pulled out the letter. It was yellowed with age and the paper felt brittle, but the writing remained clear as day. Freddie's messy scroll was scribbled all the way down the page, covering it both sides with writing.

> *My dear, my beauty, my Charlotte,* the letter began. She smiled to herself, remembering how over the top they were.
>
> *We'll be done high school soon and I know you're still trying to figure out what you want to do with your life. Don't worry. The answers to some of the most important questions we have sometimes come to us when we least expect it. Why don't we grab gelato tonight and we can look up at the moon and the stars over the Sea?*
>
> *I know I say it too much, too publically, too out of the blue, but I love you. I can't wait for us to explore the world together. When I become an F1 driver, we will travel everywhere. One day I'll propose, don't you worry. I know I'm not supposed to say that yet, but I don't care.*
>
> *I love you forever and always,*
> *Freddie xxx*

It was strange how much she had forgotten and how quickly it came back to her—the swell of emotions she once felt, still felt, and wanted to feel forever. Love was a tricky thing. Although dormant for ten years, it hadn't left. Warmth and emotion built inside of her, threatening to burst free. Freddie loved her. He always had. Who else wrote like that? Who else waited as he had? Who took in a nine-year-old?

Charlotte didn't want to leave Monaco or Freddie or Nicholas or her mémé. She really didn't want to go. She wanted to stay and be with Freddie, Nicholas, and her mémé forever. But she had learnt not to trust her emotions over the years. Now, they seemed to spill out of her like water from a tipped cup.

Perhaps there was another option other than the two she had presented herself with all this time. Maybe there was a third option.

After all, neither of the two roads she had envisioned seemed right to her. Neither sat well. That third option involved the worst part of both plans as far as how they affected her; however, it might be the best option for Freddie and Nicholas. She could tell him the truth and allow it to be an opportunity for healing, rather than just pain. The pain was inevitable, the healing was necessary. Inevitably, he would want her to leave, so she would leave. But at least Freddie and Nicholas would no longer be living a lie. It would be the start of their brand-new story. She could do whatever she needed to do to answer all of their questions. For once, the idea of being an open book felt entirely necessary.

For the first time while thinking about this, Charlotte wasn't too worried about how she would fare. It only mattered how Freddie and Nicholas responded to that news. She would have to be patient, very careful, and stop spending any more time with them until she could come face-to-face with the cold hard truth.

For once, Charlotte felt something akin to being ready. She would never *fully* be as ready as she'd like, but this was most likely as good as it got. It was the closest she had ever been. It would have to do.

Remembering her mémé's words, Charlotte still felt nowhere near confident about what she should do to start working on that fix, but at least she had a spark of an idea. And that was certainly better than nothing.

Picking up a pen, Charlotte found a piece of stationary from an old set she had when she was still in high school. She had always liked handwritten letters. Freddie had known that. That letter she had just read was one of hundreds of letters they had written back and forth, even though back then they had lived only a few blocks away from one another. He had been her knight in shining armor. She supposed that in their version of a fairytale, he was her knight in a red Ferrari.

Charlotte sighed. Perhaps their story wasn't completely over. Perhaps there was a way to help grow a beautiful and *healthy* garden, and Freddie's too, to use her grandmother's imagery. Even though it still felt impossible, Charlotte tried to imagine what it would feel like if she told Freddie the truth. Maybe it wasn't too late. Who knew what would come of it, but if healing was in the cards, she had to give it a shot. They deserved to know. It was clear as day that Freddie's foundation had some cracks in it too—maybe in Nicholas'. She would fix that. She needed to. Freddie and Nicholas' relationship was in serious need of roadside assistance to help them get to their destination... even if neither of them knew where they were going. Charlotte thought she knew just the tool to get them there. Smoothing out the page a couple of times with her palm, she took a deep breath as she put ink to the page.

Dear Freddie...

TWENTY

Freddie

A letter sat for three days in Freddie's mailbox at his condominium unnoticed. That wasn't unusual for him, since the majority of the mail he received were invitations to store openings and catalogues from which he could never seem to get taken off the subscription list. Checking his mailbox was the furthest thing from his mind.

He was too busy helping Nicholas with his rehabilitation, driving the kid to and from school, and doing his best to distract himself from his broken heart. It wasn't easy doing it all, feeling like his insides had been wrenched out of him. How had he fallen for her so hard, again? And how had she slipped through his fingertips, again? He was certain he wasn't imagining their connection.

He had put it all on the line. He had risked it all. Now, he had blown it. He'd sped in a construction zone and now he had a flat tire. He was going nowhere thanks to his behavior. He could kick himself if he could. He didn't know if it was the proposal or them moving too fast? *In hindsight, it had probably been the proposal*, he thought. How stupid was he to think that he could rush things? To think that if only they were married, that it would solve all of those problems? He wished he had never seen that ring. He pulled it out of his shorts pocket, examining the way that the light bounced off of the diamonds in a million directions.

Freddie's new sailboat, the Sea Grand Prix, was docked right where he had left it. She was a beauty and Freddie had spent the few months leading up to the sale learning everything about sailboats. Christian was waiting for him at the dock.

"Man, you look awful," Christian teased as Freddie approached, wearing his wetsuit and carrying his scuba gear in his hand.

"Not as bad as you're going to look after I push you in," Freddie said with more of an edge than he meant.

"Hey, I was just kidding," Christian said, lifting up his hands as if to surrender.

Everything he could have beaten himself up over, he already had. He had lost her once and now he had lost her again, presumably forever this time. Besides, if Charlotte had wanted to reach him, she knew where she could find him. He wasn't about to start reaching out to her again. The ball was in her court. Besides, he had already given her an advantage, if she still wanted to play that game, and he hadn't left his condominium much over the last few days just in case she stopped by. She never did. Her phone number hadn't come through on his cell phone either. Not a single text message. Ultimately, if she had changed her mind, she would have reached out. If she had wanted to talk, she would have. She was in the driver's seat. Her actions were speaking loud and clear: clearly she wanted things to be over and he had to respect that.

Freddie still hadn't told Christian about the proposal gone wrong. He hadn't told a soul, not even Nicholas. As long as he kept it a secret, he could handle it. As long as he didn't talk about it, it wasn't real. The pain could remain dulled, his brain foggy, and the sting of a broken heart not yet fully felt. He knew he could die with that secret, but he had an inkling of a suspicion that talking about it might help.

After all, what was the worst that could happen? Charlotte had already turned him down. Facing his feelings certainly wouldn't make them worse. *Probably.*

"So, how are things going with you and Charlotte?" Christian asked in a teasing tone. "We'd love to have the two of you over for dinner. Maybe a double date? What do you think?"

He definitely needed to tell Christian. "Well…"

Christian threw the supplies onto the boat before throwing up his hands. "Don't tell me, you asked her to marry you?"

Freddie frowned. "How did you know?"

Christian burst into laughter. "Hah. Nicholas mentioned it the last time we were at the track. Said you two had bought a ring. But you should have seen your face, thinking I was psychic or something…"

"More like *psycho*," Freddie teased. He cursed himself for having been so naive as to bring Nicholas into the plans by allowing him to help pick the ring. But then again, that had been the plan. The three of them together. At least, that's the plan his foolish mind had concocted.

"So, what happened?" Christian prodded.

"Well…"

He spilled it all to Christian as he threw his equipment into the boat, just trying to say the words as accurately and devoid of emotion as possible. As usual, Christian listened calmly, not saying a word. Freddie found himself admitting things he hadn't even known he felt.

"I'm swerving out of control, man. Who proposes after such a short period of time?" Freddie finally asked.

Christian smiled sadly. "Someone in love, my friend. Someone in love."

"I'm lucky to have Nicholas around," Freddie said. "Never thought I would be saying that to be totally honest, but I'm sure you understand that."

Nicholas had been a huge distraction for the past three days. And even though Nicholas seemed to have talked about it to Christian, the kid hadn't mentioned the upcoming proposal since they had bought that three-diamond ring. That boy seemed to be a ray of sunshine in his rainy life. Even with his broken arm, the two of them energetically discussed racing strategies and tactics. The night before, their conversation had taken a deeper turn as Nicholas divulged to him his feelings about his parents' death—the shock, the sadness, and the occasional anger that came up.

"It still feels a bit like a dream sometimes," Nicholas had told him with a shrug. "I don't really know how I feel all the time. Driving helps though. All my thoughts are clear. It's like a sky that was filled with clouds before, and becomes totally blue the second my foot hits the gas pedal."

Freddie had known exactly what Nicholas meant. The next day while Nicholas was at school, Freddie needed that mental clarity. He needed those clouds to clear. There was only one thing that was going to help.

Racing was no longer much of an option, and he certainly didn't feel quite as anonymous at the karting track as he needed to be… not to mention that it was mostly filled with kids. He couldn't just race an F1 car anymore—he was retired. That ship had sailed. But there was one place Freddie found himself thinking about. One place where he could get total and complete peace.

The waves around him and Christian crashed against the dock and the Sea Grand Prix swayed in the breeze. Nearby seagulls swooped from the skies, cawing and spreading their wings. The sea air was good for him. It had a miraculous ability to make even the foggiest of minds feel clear.

"Nicholas is a great kid," Christian agreed. "He's lucky to have you."

Freddie scoffed as he climbed into the boat.

Christian persisted. "I'm serious. I don't know why on Earth those nutty Stefanos left their only kid to you, but I'm glad they did. They clearly saw something in you. Even I, as your appointed best friend, wouldn't have guessed that fatherhood would suit you so well."

"I'm not his dad," Freddie was quick to clarify.

"No, that's true. But you're not *just* his guardian either."

Freddie shook his head. "He really took to Charlotte. You know, I couldn't help but think that it was all coming together. I couldn't help but think that the universe had some grand plan for us, bringing me, Nicholas, and Charlotte together at the same time. I was so silly thinking that she was the final piece to the puzzle. But it's just me and Nicholas."

Christian clapped Freddie on the back. "Man, what is it about her? There's just something about the two of you. You never seem to get the timing right. I thought you would know more than anyone else—timing is everything."

Freddie managed a smile. "Yeah, just bad timing," he agreed. Of course, Freddie knew there was so much more to it than that. But he had already shared so much more than he had intended. He was desperate to shift gears.

"You ready?" Christian asked, as they pulled out of the marina and hit the open sea. "You can drive. I'm going to get our gear sorted."

Freddie breathed in the fresh sea air, taking the wheel in his hands, and steered the boat into the vast blue abyss. Already, he was feeling lighter with more physical distance placed between him and Monaco and with more space between him and Charlotte.

Scuba diving was a new hobby for Freddie. As an F1 driver, he hadn't had as much time to devote to the hobby as he would have liked. But now that he was retired, he could do what he wanted. It helped that Christian was a water-nut. Anything snorkeling, scuba, or boating related and Christian was there. It was Christian's mission to dive the greatest spots in the world and had already flown to Australia exclusively to dive the Great Barrier Reef.

Once they were out a far enough distance, Freddie dropped anchor and their boat came to a standstill. He walked carefully to put on his scuba gear, careful not to fall from the steady rocking of the boat.

For the first time in the past three days, Freddie took a deep breath of salty air and felt something deep within him unclench. Relaxing ever so slightly to the force of the sea. It was like doing two-hours of yoga without the work. Nothing seemed to heal a wounded heart quite as well as the sea; of course, except for Charlotte herself.

The only sound was the wind whipping against the sails and the waves lapping at the boat. Just him and his best friend. Solitude was exactly what he needed.

"Hey, you two!"

A voice, high-pitched and forceful, pierced his eardrums over the sound of the water, breaking his meditative state. A tiny shiver ran up his spine. It couldn't be.

Freddie turned to see a small boat approaching, a familiar face and waving hands. He squinted his eyes, thinking that his mind must be playing tricks on him. *No, no, no, no, no.* Hadn't he already been through enough over these past few days?

It was Violet. But not just Violet, *because that would have been too easy*, Freddie thought. She was protected and surrounded by her gaggle of girlfriends who Freddie would have rather avoided. Seeming to have new friends almost weekly, he recalled that she had never had much luck at maintaining friendships. As the other boat drew nearer, it was just as he thought. Not a familiar face except for his ex-girlfriend. Only Violet could yell loud enough to pierce through the sound of the waves.

He couldn't escape. He needed airbags just to breathe in Monaco, there seemed to be so many hazards everywhere he went. Looking to Christian, he pulled a face. Christian was looking from left to right, as if there was a plausible place to go. But they had already dropped anchor. Their boat wasn't going anywhere right now. It wasn't exactly like he could pretend he hadn't heard and dive into the sea; he was nowhere near ready to get his dive suit and gear on. Christian glanced at him quizzically as he zipped up his wetsuit. There really was no way to avoid it. Why was it that the one woman he wanted was nowhere in sight and the one he wanted nothing to do with was now about to... board his new boat?

The small boat, complete with a captain, had stopped dangerously close to his own sailboat. He kept one eye on the distance between the boats and the other on Violet, who was stumbling slightly as she climbed up the ladder to the dock. With a glazed and happy expression on her face, her friends remained on their own boat. Freddie caught a glimpse of a sash, a few bottles of champagne, and suddenly Violet's eagerness to jump aboard his ship made sense.

She was drunk.

With a crown perched atop her head, she staggered over to him. "Freddie! Freddie, Freddie, Freddie," she said, slurring her words.

Christian stood at the edge, carefully watching that their adjacent one didn't scratch up the Sea Grand Prix.

"What are you doing?" Freddie asked, not bothering to keep the agitation from his voice.

"What, you don't want to see me?" Violet asked, hiccupping. On her sash, the word *Bride* was bedazzled in pink.

"You're getting married, I see?" Freddie asked, amusement creeping into his tone.

"Jealous?" Violet asked, putting her hand on her jutted out hip.

The jostling waves made her sway from side to side. Freddie wondered if she even noticed. "No, ma'am," Freddie said, a slight smile forming on his face.

"Well, I just came to tell you that this is your last chance," Violet continued, her voice rising. "You know, you ended things so quickly. I don't think you really thought things through—"

"All right, which one of you lovely ladies wants to help the bride back onto her boat?" Freddie called to Violet's friends. They burst into fits of laughter. Freddie looked to Christian for help, but he was trying to get the hired driver of their vessel to move away from their own boat so they wouldn't crash. The hired driver looked unconcerned. He needed to take back control of the situation before they crashed and burned.

Violet stuck out her bottom lip. "You don't even care that I'm getting married, do you?"

Freddie sighed. "No, Violet. Frankly, I don't. We're over. It was over the second you called the reporter the *first* time."

Violet's eyes flashed. "Well, you seem awfully taken by Charlotte. Strange how she seems to have popped up again out of nowhere, after you end up adopting that kid."

There was a fire burning in Freddie. Alarm bells were signaling with Violet, there was always smoke before detectable flames. "You don't know what you're talking about," Freddie said in even tones.

"Strange how she left in such a flash, isn't it? Ten years ago? And how old is Freddie exactly? Nine? He certainly bears an uncanny resemblance to you, Freddie. I'd do a paternity test if I were you—"

"—Violet, you're talking crazy. Seriously, I don't need a—"

"—Freddie! The captain has agreed to leave," Christian called out, as he emptied his wallet and handed over a stack of bills.

Violet smiled and flicked her hair. "Well, I should be going. Delightful seeing you, Freddie. *Do* send me and my soon-to-be-husband a wedding card."

Freddie had just been ambushed. As Violet held onto Christian's hand and hopped back onto her own boat, her own friends cheered as they jetted off without so much as a glance backwards.

"That girl knows no limits," Christian said, laughing nervously. "I knew it when you were together, but I didn't think she was that… uh… *confident.*"

The words that Violet had said echoed through his mind. She had planted a seed. A vicious seed—the kind that strangles all the surrounding greenery. His anxiety turbocharged, he couldn't scuba dive. He couldn't clear his mind. He had to find Charlotte and fast. He needed to know: was Nicholas his son?

TWENTY-ONE

Charlotte

The letter had been written and sent days ago. Not a word. Not a peep from him. She wondered if he was silently seething. He certainly would never want to talk to her again. That much was clear. Staying in Monaco felt impossible. With her grandmother's blessing and confirmation that she was doing just fine, Charlotte had to leave. No point sticking around, creating further hurt. If Freddie had wanted to talk, if he had any questions for her, he would have reached out to her.

You need to check-in on him. Even if he doesn't want to see you, he needs to know you care.

The voice in her head was crystal clear. She had already reconciled that he wouldn't want her to stay, but Nicholas would inevitably have questions. She needed to give Freddie the answers. And she would follow Freddie's lead about how to handle it with Nicholas. She owed him and Nicholas at least that much.

A plan had already been formulated in her mind. She would go to visit with Freddie—even wait at his apartment if he didn't answer his phone. But she needed to look him in the eye and say one thing: "I am so sorry. I am just so sorry."

She would never be able to live with herself without saying

those words. And if he didn't want her to tell Nicholas, she would never be able to say those words to him aloud. But she would say them everyday to herself, just as she already was. *I'm sorry. I'm sorry. I'm sorry.*

Guilt was a curious emotion, one that she was numb to for many years. An influx of "what if's" had been plaguing her and it meant she hadn't gotten a wink of sleep since sending the letter. Anxiously, she had kept one eye on her phone at all hours in case somehow the volume, which was turned to full-blast, stopped working. Of course, none of that mattered. Freddie hadn't wanted to see her. He could have reached out. The ball was in his court.

Her flight was booked for the following evening. If she didn't speak to him now, when would she ever talk to him? She couldn't leave without knowing for sure. She needed to say those words. A small glimmer of hope, so small it was barely a spark, lingered in her mind.

Maybe I can be a part of their lives. Maybe I can watch Nicholas grow up, even if from afar.

She wasn't holding out hope. It was understandable if Freddie never wanted to speak to her again. But in her mind, nothing was a total write-off until he told her so explicitly. She needed to apologize, answer any questions he had, and finally see if there was any room for her to remain in Nicholas' life. It was a big *if.*

As for Freddie's proposal? She had thought about it every moment since. She couldn't stop replaying the memory in her mind. Second to one particular memory and moment in time, that was both the hardest and happiest moment of her life. It made her realize what she wanted and what she didn't want. A part of her wanted to have it all—the husband, the son, the reunited family, the laughter, happiness, and memories. She knew that would never be possible but it was a nice fantasy.

What she didn't want wielded far more power over her. She didn't want to create hurt, pain, or anger even more than she already had. Her mémé's words echoed in her mind again—perhaps starting from the ground up and re-building her foundation was possible. But she would never know for sure without talking to Freddie.

Charlotte was a patient woman, but over those past few days had grown restless. She couldn't bear to wait any longer and made her way to Freddie's apartment. He wasn't answering his phone. She needed to see him. Although she turned out to be able to spend ten years apart, the time between them over the past three days felt acutely painful.

She bit her lip as she stood outside of his apartment, trying his phone once again. Nothing. Straight to voicemail. Panic bubbled up inside her. Perhaps this was how things ended. Maybe she would never see Freddie again. Maybe her time with Nicholas was over. Maybe this was their story, their ending—

"—Charlotte?"

Mid-thought, she turned to see a red-faced Freddie walking towards her with determination. Her heart fluttered. Him. It was Freddie. So this wasn't the end of their story. Relief washed over her momentarily before the fear flooded her fully. His eyes flashed. Alone and with determination in his pace, this was no ordinary meeting.

"Freddie, I'm so glad to see you. I'm so—"

"—Is it true?" Freddie blurted out.

With her heart pounding, her thoughts turning to mush, and her legs threatening to give out beneath her, this was the moment she had dreaded her entire adult life. It was finally here, staring her in the face. She didn't need the question spelled out for her. His face said it all—twisted, angst-filled, angry, and ultimately heartbroken. She knew that expression. It had looked back at her in the mirror for years. Time had faded some of that pain, making the edges fuzzy and the memory a little softer. But now it was back in its rawest form. Freddie had a desperate air about him—*needing* to know anything had that effect on people. It wasn't just a question. Charlotte knew that this moment was as hard for him as it was for her.

She took a step towards him, reaching out with one hand, trying to place it on his chest. Immediately he took a step back. He was cloaked in mistrust.

"Charlotte," Freddie tried again, his voice down to a near

whisper. "Is Nicholas my s—"

As his face broke, the agony of the situation crushing him with each second, it was clear he couldn't get the words out. He couldn't even say the word 'son'. Charlotte wished she could do anything to take that pain away. Tears springing to her eyes, a pit in her stomach and a crushing sensation to her lungs, her vision tunneled to see just him and only him.

"I'm sorry," she gasped. Her brain was telling her to say a million other things. *Tell him again. Tell him what happened. Tell him the truth.* But her lip quivered and a tear fell onto her cheek, words remaining unspoken. The two of them stood in silence unbearably, but uttering another word felt completely impossible.

"And you didn't think to tell me?" Freddie said, hurt dripping in his tone.

Charlotte's eyes widened. "The letter explained everything—"

"—Look, I don't know anything about a letter," Freddie continued. He paced back and forth, his eyes darting from one thing to another. "I can't believe you didn't tell me."

Charlotte felt near to sobbing. How had he not read the letter? How could that be possible? "I did tell you. It's all in the letter. I wrote everything for you... what happened, why, and I tried to answer any more obvious questions that you might have had—"

"—I have to go," Freddie said abruptly.

With a surge of adrenaline, Charlotte looked up to meet his eyes. Her whole body felt chilled. "Wait, don't go—"

"—I have to," he replied with harshness in his voice. Charlotte tried to see his soul, but his eyes were vacant. "I need to pick up my, *our*, son... you know, I have to go."

Freddie turned on his heel, walking in the other direction. He walked right past his own car, which Charlotte noticed was parked further down the street.

Her legs felt like lead was poured into them. There was no chasing after him, no dramatics. She wished that they could go wheel-to-wheel. An argument, a fight, *anything* would have been better than steely silence. The world continued on, a couple passing by her holding hands. No one knew what had just happened. No one except for the two of them. Her breathing coming in heaves. All of her worst nightmares, the worst-case scenario had come true. There was an abundance of hurt. But more than hurt, there was anger. She hadn't known how to respond to that, although it made total sense to her. More curiously, somehow he had found out about Nicholas. But he clearly hadn't found out from her.

Nothing about this was neat, shiny, or tidy.

Yet another mistake she had made. She hadn't told Freddie the news the right way or soon enough. *Stupid girl*, she chastised herself. When was she going to learn?

Charlotte had a million questions running through her mind, but one stuck out in particular: who told Freddie?

TWENTY-TWO

Freddie

W*hat letter?* Freddie ran home to his condominium, forgetting entirely about his car. He felt frantic and frazzled. His head felt like it was about to explode. The letter. He needed to read that letter. Upon arriving at his condo, he ran to the mailroom, where he had only been a handful of times before, and located the mail key on his key fob. Opening it, letters poured out. He should have done this a lot sooner.

He couldn't think of anything else. If he did, he didn't know what would happen. Was it possible to collapse due to shock? He didn't want to find out. Rummaging through them with shaking hands, he eventually found the one with Charlotte's neat scrawl. He tore it open immediately.

Dear Freddie, the letter began. *I'm sorry...*

He read the entire thing twice over, and then once more because he couldn't help himself. The letter broke his heart, reaching places inside of him he didn't know he could ache. It made him angry, stirring up inside of him questions that needed answers. Shedding light on everything he could have possibly had questions for, Charlotte had told him why she left Monaco, how much she had wanted him to thrive in his career and have the success he had always dreamt of, why she chose the Stefanos, why she left for New York City, and why she hadn't told him. The truth stirred every emotion inside of him. There was only so long that one could remain in that state of intensity, and now he felt depleted and worried. Worried about Nicholas, worried about Charlotte, and worried about himself. Although Charlotte had been thorough with her letter, he needed to hear it from her. He still had questions for her—things that felt they couldn't wait. Still, the idea of moving from the mailroom and facing the real world felt nearly impossible. Simply taking one breath after another seemed to be all he could do.

"Excuse me, are you okay?"

Freddie looked up to see the concierge, staring at him with a concerned expression. He must have been standing in that mailroom for a half hour at least.

"I'm fine, thank you," Freddie said, bristling as he wished that he had total privacy.

"I wanted to let you know that your son is here," the concierge said.

Freddie hadn't bothered explaining the whole Nicholas situation to anyone in his building, including the concierge. It made sense that they assumed Nicholas was his son. He felt shocked hearing those words though, wishing he could douse his entire life in coolant. Before reading that letter, the assumption would have rolled off of him, since the words meant nothing other than someone else's error. Now, they held a world of meaning.

Freddie peered through the glass door to see Nicholas sitting in the lobby, his head down and staring at his shoes. His heart broke open, fragments of every emotion spilling out and into him simultaneously.

That was his son. Not just any kid. His *son*. He loved that kid, even if he wasn't biologically his. But he was.

"Thank you," he muttered to the concierge before dashing through those doors towards Nicholas. His son. He wanted to weep.

Nicholas didn't know a thing. He hadn't even begun to think about what he should tell Nicholas, he had been so wrapped up in trying to process the information.

He wanted to ask Nicholas: "What's wrong?" but he held his tongue. He knew that even in the worst-case scenario, panicking in front of him would never help. Instead, he took a steadying breath.

"Hey kid," he said, his voice a little shakier than he would have liked. To Nicholas, this was just another day. Any other day. He just needed to act normal. He placed his hand on his hip, jutting it out at an angle.

"Why are you standing so weird?" Nicholas asked, his face screwed up as he looked upwards.

Freddie shook out his arm, feigning nonchalance. "Oh, nothing, just standing normally."

"Okay..."

"You're home early," Freddie added quickly, trying to change the subject.

Nicholas looked up, his cheeks red and blotchy.

"I was lied to, Freddie."

Freddie's heart sank into his stomach. The hurt in Nicholas' eyes stirred up feelings in him he had never before felt. It was inevitable that Nicholas would find out eventually, but this was too soon. Even Freddie hadn't had time to fully process it yet. He didn't want to make more of a mess of the situation than it already was.

"Okay, I can try to explain," he fumbled, panic rising up in him like bubbles in a champagne glass.

Nicholas pouted, looking away from Freddie again. "She doesn't like me, or at least, not according to Markus. Apparently *he's* taking her on a date. He was throwing it in my face at lunch and I just couldn't take it anymore."

Scanning his mind, Freddie was drawing a blank. What was the kid talking about? He certainly didn't know. Markus? A girl who didn't like him? It dawned on him suddenly. A huge weight had fallen off of him. He stifled an inadvertent, incredulous laugh as a cough. Nicholas had no idea about this big secret. At least, not yet.

"Oh, oh right. Miranda, was it? She's that girl in your class you like?" Freddie felt delighted he had remembered the name of Nicholas' crush *and* that disaster was averted. At least he was handling something well.

"No, I don't like her. I *love* her," Nicholas said solemnly.

Freddie wanted to roll his eyes good-naturedly but he restrained himself. Poor Nicholas was such a sensitive kid. And he was his *son*. Who would have ever known he would have such an emotionally intelligent child? He felt like he was looking at him with an entirely new perspective. He had to fight the urge to hug the kid. Although he still felt on edge, that initial twinge of panic was wearing off. He felt he could breathe a bit easier.

As he sat down on the white leather sofa next to Nicholas in the lobby, it was suddenly like he was seeing that kid for the very first time. This was his son. His *son*. He still couldn't believe it. Those similarities that Christian had mentioned weren't all in his friend's head. Freddie searched Nicholas' face for resemblances.

"Why are you looking at me funny?" Nicholas asked suspiciously.

Freddie shook his head quickly. "Oh nothing, nothing at all. So, what are you going to do?" Freddie heard himself saying.

"I don't know," Nicholas moaned.

Freddie sighed. "There's the stuff we can't control—in this case, that's Markus. We can't control how he reacts or what he says. It sounds like he's not such a nice guy. And then there's the stuff we can control—how we treat people, in this case, Miranda. Do you see what I'm getting at?"

Freddie felt chuffed at authentically giving his first tidbit of fatherly wisdom. His first bit of fatherly advice. He thought that he was taking to the new role quite well. He was a natural, *probably*. Glowing his pride, he beamed at Nicholas as he awaited his son's response.

"I should punch Markus?" Nicholas ventured.

Freddie burst out laughing, shaking his head. "No, *no*. I don't know how you got that from what I said."

Maybe he still needed to hone his instincts just a tad.

Nicholas smiled slightly. "I know, I was just teasing you. I know what you're saying."

Freddie felt like his heart was going to explode. Here he was—sitting with his son in his beautiful apartment lobby in Monaco, joking around and imparting wisdom. He had every reason to feel overwhelmed, angry, scared, happy, or stuck. But he only felt incredibly blessed. He wished that he could tell Nicholas everything. He wanted it all out in the open. A protective instinct ensured that his lips remained sealed.

"My original plan was to impress Miranda at the karting track. We were going to do a field trip there in a few weeks. She would see me as the fastest driver and then fall in love."

Freddie frowned. "Well, you're getting your cast off in not too long, what's the problem?"

Nicholas ran his good hand along the cast. "I—I don't know. I guess I'm a bit nervous about getting back in the go-kart."

Freddie nodded. "A healthy dose of fear after an injury, especially the kind you sustained, is normal. Some people might tell you they're never afraid, but don't listen to those people. Those people are the liars."

"Like Markus."

"Exactly," Freddie said enthusiastically, not quite sure how Markus was a liar, but Nicholas seemed fired up and in a better mood.

"So what's the plan? What's within my control?" Nicholas asked, his eyes shining and filled with hope.

Freddie fumbled, not sure what to say. He didn't want to disappoint Nicholas and say the wrong thing. "How about we get you an extra physiotherapy appointment and book an appointment with your doctor to see when you can get back in a go-kart?" He crossed his fingers he had said the right thing.

Nicholas smiled ear to ear. "Brilliant," he said, hopping to his feet. "D'you want to get a gelato now? Gelato always makes me feel better."

Freddie matched Nicholas' enthusiasm. "Absolutely. Of course."

Although he had been Nicholas' guardian for weeks and a biological father for the last nine years, he only really felt like a *parent* at that moment. He had been given the jumpstart he needed. That moment when he did his best to help the kid solve a problem. Suppressing the rage that bubbled up thinking of Nicholas in pain. Controlling his emotions to be the best person he could be and set a good example for Nicholas. Parenting was a lot harder than he had thought. He didn't want to miss another second of it.

TWENTY-THREE

Charlotte

Who, who, *who*? Charlotte had never been one for mysteries. She didn't watch crime TV shows or have any interest in playing detective as a child. There was nothing fun about trying to solve this problem. Even though she didn't feel particular adept, she had a sneaking suspicion of who might have told Freddie.

Walking to her mémé's bedroom door, she knocked carefully, her heart racing. "Can I talk to you for a second?"

"Of course, come in *ma cherie*," her mémé called from inside.

Her mémé's bedroom smelled of roses and talc. Although the room had windows that exhibited the magnificent oceanfront view, the heavy white curtains were drawn. Her mémé was sitting on a tufted armchair, the soft glow of her lamp beside her, and a book in her hand. It was the usual afternoon routine her mémé had developed since the fall.

Charlotte wrung her hands. "You didn't happen to tell anyone about Nicholas, did you?" she asked, her voice a couple octaves higher than usual as she braced herself for friction.

Her mémé shut her book and looked at her seriously. "No, I did not. That's not information anyone should know."

Charlotte nodded slowly. "Right, I thought so. I *knew* so. I just needed to hear it from you. I was wondering, do you think Isabelle and Roland told anyone?"

"No. No, I do not."

"How come?" Charlotte persisted. At her core, she knew that neither Isabelle nor Roland would have whispered the secret to anyone. But she needed to hear it.

"They loved Nicholas more than anything in the world," her mémé said crisply. "When the adoption took place, they promised me they would never utter a word about it again. They didn't want to hurt Nicholas."

To Charlotte, the truth suddenly seemed like it wasn't a huge deal. She had gotten pregnant and provided two loving parents-to-be with a child. It was as if she could breathe fresh air for the first time. For years, she had beaten herself up. It was the price she deserved to pay, she had convinced herself. Now, there was the creeping suspicion to Charlotte that it was the secrecy of it all that had become tormenting. It was hiding the truth beneath the surface, where it was always lurking. Not a birthday, celebration, or holiday went by without that truth haunting her, toiling in her mind and poisoning her happiness. It wasn't the truth itself—Nicholas was a blessing. It was always having to hide.

Although she wanted to know who had told Freddie, a part of her thought it honestly didn't matter anymore. She had written him that letter. The truth would have come out one way or another. Maybe someone had gotten to the letter before him. Maybe someone had blabbed. Who knew? But if another person knew, so be it. Right now, the only thing that mattered was finding Freddie.

"I have to go," Charlotte said breathlessly, grabbing her purse on the way out the door.

She didn't know what had gotten into her. For the first time in ten years, she could breathe. The truth was out there, flowing freely like the wind through the Monaco streets. She needed to find Freddie and apologize—for the lies. She wanted it to stop there. She *needed* it to stop there. She was a V8 engine with no signs of slowing down.

"Well, I seem to be running into you just everywhere," came a voice.

A few feet ahead of her stood Violet. She had been so focused on getting to Freddie's apartment she hadn't noticed the fashionably dressed woman taking a selfie. She veered to a stop.

"Nice to see you again," she said breathlessly. "I'm afraid I'm in a bit of a hurry—"

"Off to see Freddie, are you?"

Charlotte turned back to see Violet smirking at her. She was swaying slightly, barely masking her minor hiccups that came up every few seconds.

It dawned on Charlotte that she was wearing a sash and tiara. Her eyes narrowed. "How did you know?" she asked slowly, turning to give Violet her full attention.

Violet seemed to relish in it and flipped her hair. "Oh, just a guess. The two of you just can't seem to keep your hands off of each other. Plus, I figured you would be heading over, what to spend time as a *family* and all."

Alarm bells were going off in Charlotte's brain. Violet. It was Violet.

"Family?" Charlotte heard herself echo, her voice surprisingly steady.

Violet appeared momentarily frazzled. "I'm just taking a closer look at the situation," she said with a hiccup.

Charlotte walked up to Violet so she was dangerously close. "Listen here," she growled. "I don't know what your game is, but I get the feeling that you think you know something. Well, let me tell you, you could ruin someone's life with the words you're spouting."

Violet shrunk in her high heels, eyes wide. "I'm sorry," Violet blurted. "I'm sorry. I mean, I didn't actually think it's true… is it?"

To Charlotte's horror and astonishment, Violet's eyes welled with tears.

"Freddie and I had the best relationship," Violet slurred before hiccupping again. "And I'm getting married in a week's time. I've been trying to get his attention for ages since he broke up with me, but nothing. Then you come along..." Violet was practically wailing at this point.

Charlotte needed to get her off of the street. The noise was starting to draw heads.

"Where are your friends?" Charlotte asked frantically. Surely her bachelorette group couldn't be too far away.

"Oh, they all left," Violet said, tears now streaming silently down her face. "They aren't my real friends anyway. I don't have many of those. One of them I met last week. They're the wives of my future husband-to-be." She spoke between sobs. In her high heels, sash, and mascara-streaked face, Violet didn't look like the menacing, mean girl that Charlotte had pegged her as. Violet was a total mess.

Only a few hours earlier, Charlotte would have relished in it. But now, there was a twinge of something softening in her. To her, Violet was the worst kind of person: the kind that actively seemed to go out of their way to hurt others. She was a lemon hiding under a 'mint condition' body. Whatever Violet had said to Freddie had clearly had an impact. The anger and fury were still blazing in her. But after seeing Violet up close, those were accompanied by a different emotion.

Charlotte took a deep breath, thinking there was a very good chance that she would regret what she was about to do. "Violet, would you like to come up to my apartment? Get yourself cleaned up a bit? Have a cup of tea?" She knew what Violet really needed was a strong cup of coffee and a long nap.

Violet blew her nose onto her dress sleeve. "All right," she finally said quietly. "Yes, I think that would be okay."

Charlotte helped Violet clip-clop in her high heels all the way to her Le Soleil, where even the concierge gave her a surprised look. The two women could not have looked more different—one in a minidress, mascara-stained cheeks, mile-high heels and a sash, and the other in a matching taupe-colored linen pants and shirt set. When she finally got Violet upstairs, Violet was confiding to her all her secrets. Charlotte was doing her best to change the subject—anything to stop her from telling her more. But Violet continued like a high-speed train. There was no stopping her.

"...and then in high school, I cheated on my final exams. I hired someone to come in and take the tests. I know I shouldn't have. I pretended I got these amazing grades, and when I got to university, I was hopeless. I think I have dyslexia, but I've never been tested..."

Charlotte opened the door to the apartment, got Violet settled inside on the leather sofa, and began making a pot of coffee.

"...I don't know about this whole marriage business. Some people make it look so easy. And why does Yanic even love me? Sure, we have fun together, but is that love? I don't know..."

She was only half listening when her mémé stepped out of her bedroom, laid eyes on Violet, and raised her eyebrows in silence to Charlotte. Charlotte shrugged and pulled a face. What else could she do?

"Here," she said to Violet, thrusting a cup of strong coffee. "Drink this."

Violet was still rambling between sips. When Charlotte went to refill her mug, she returned to her guest sleeping on the sofa, her body draped along the length of the entire couch. A faint snoring sound was emitted from her as her chest rose and fell with each breath.

Her mémé exited from her hiding place in her bedroom. "Well, you've made quite the friend," she said in a teasing tone.

"Not a friend," Charlotte said. She felt sorry for Violet, who was lying asleep on her sofa at the end of her very own bachelorette party. At least in that moment, all of Charlotte's anger and hatred had been put on pause.

"She's quite a sight," her mémé mused, grabbing a cup of coffee for herself. By now, her mémé was managing with a limp but no longer relied on her cane.

"She's Freddie's ex," Charlotte explained. "She sold a bunch of his private information to the press while they were dating. Obviously, he ended things with her. I guess she was pretty upset. She concocted the whole Freddie-Nicholas debacle to get back at him. I don't think she actually believes a word of what she's spewed," she said calmly. To her own surprise, she felt calm. She sipped her coffee thoughtfully. "I think she's the one who told Freddie. She hasn't said it, but it's more than clear..."

Her mémé patted her hand. "My dear, you are a very patient soul."

Charlotte smiled. "No, I'm not. I just understand what she's going through. I think she's trying to pretend to be perfect and the lies are accumulating in her attempt to hide the truth. If I were to judge her for that, I'd be a hypocrite."

"Well," Marguerite managed. "That's quite..."

Charlotte gave her mémé a kiss on the cheek. It wasn't up to her grandmother to understand this complicated emotional mess she was going through.

She wondered if Violet would be in this position if the poor girl had ever been provided with some words of affirmation like her mémé gave to her. Charlotte never took her mémé for granted, having grown up with the parents she had. If she hadn't had such a stable figure to fall back on, who knew how she would have become—perhaps someone not so far from Violet.

"I need to go," Charlotte said. "She'll probably be out like a light for at least a few hours. I need to go find Freddie."

Her mémé looked seriously into her eyes. "Go make things right, *ma belle*."

Charlotte nodded, a ripple of self-assurance running through her. "I will. Don't worry, I will."

TWENTY-FOUR

Freddie

Freddie felt like he had just run a marathon—except instead of feeling a runner's high, he felt completely emotionally spent. Nicholas was at his physiotherapy appointment. The sling and cast had come off. The kid had looked elated. Although his arm and shoulder still needed a lot of work to get back to the former strength, Nicholas was young, healthy, and ambitious. The doctor thought that the recovery wouldn't be a problem and to check-in again in two weeks.

Now alone with his thoughts, Freddie could finally focus on the problems that kept popping up in his mind. What was he going to do about Nicholas? What was he going to do about Charlotte?

He walked through the Jardins Saint-Martin, which had always been one of his favorite spots in Monaco. Native Mediterranean and exotic plants and trees were planted along the series of winding paths. Now dusk, the sun was setting beneath the sea. The air, fragrant with flowers and salt, reminded him of simpler times. Even a few hours ago, his life had felt simple by comparison.

His own advice—to his *son*—echoed in his mind. *Focus on what is within your control.* This situation seemed beyond his control. It seemed like it was gaining speed every second, getting further and further from his reach. But right now, he could focus on helping Nicholas get to his optimal health in order to get him back in a race car, he could focus on how and if he would tell Nicholas the truth, and he could focus on what he was going to say to Charlotte—Nicholas' biological mother.

That fear of failure popped up again, but this time, he felt more aware of it than scared. That fear of failure had stopped him from racing another year. That fear of failure had stopped him from chasing after Charlotte when he had the chance. That fear of failure had materialized when Charlotte said 'no' to his proposal and when he found out he was a father. He was still standing. He was still here. He was still ready to fight another fight and take another shot at a win.

He had dreamed that he would have a family one-day. This certainly hadn't been how he imagined it. This hadn't been how he had ever imagined his life to turn out. The only thing in his life that had gone according to plan was his F1 career, but even that had taken a bunch of bumps and twists along the way. Perhaps he ought to give up the idea of what his future would look like altogether. He certainly didn't feel very good at predicting it.

He stifled an incredulous laugh; it was almost unbelievable. In Charlotte's letter, the words she wrote made him think that she would never forgive herself for how everything turned out. Was he angry? Yes. Shocked? Of course. But did he think that she was undeserving of forgiveness? No.

Freddie thought that this wound would take time to heal—probably years. Maybe a lifetime. He hoped it wouldn't take that long. He also thought that a mistake wasn't a mistake if put right. Here she was, doing her best to make things right. It was incomprehensible to him how she must be feeling right now.

He had been so brash with her earlier. Of course, that was when he was operating under the assumption that Charlotte was planning on hiding the secret. Perhaps even exploiting it, with Violet's expertise. But he had it all wrong. Charlotte seemed to have been trying to tell him the truth in the best way she could. Clearly she was scared. Trying to put himself in her shoes, he imagined he would have been too.

Imagine how she must be feeling, Freddie wondered. *After how I acted, she must be terrified she'll never see Nicholas again.*

As he had read and understood in Charlotte's letter, she worried that the words wouldn't come out of her mouth if she tried to tell him in person. She worried that nothing would end up being said, or worse, that she would be so overcome with fear that she would *never* speak about it again. Although writing a letter was far easier than speaking to him in person, to her it was the only way to clearly state what had happened without emotion getting in her way. She felt so ashamed. Devastated and heartbroken, she couldn't live with herself seeing the pain it would inevitably cause him. She also couldn't bear to keep it hidden any longer, knowing that the pain of finding out the truth would be overshadowed by the joy of him having found his son.

His *son.* He could still barely wrap his head around it.

Surprisingly, he hadn't felt angry towards her when he read the letter—that had come later. At the moment, he had been flooded with sadness. Deep, heartbreaking and aching sadness that filled his chest and crevices of his heart he hadn't known existed. For her to feel that alone that young. For her to have carried this with her for so long. For her to come back and see the situation they were in now. And a part of him didn't know how he felt, with an ever-changing flow of emotions that he would inevitably need to work out with a professional.

After having had time to read the letter, Freddie had come to a conclusion—one that made sense for Charlotte but most importantly for Nicholas. He had to find her and tell her that they would figure out the next steps together—a united front as Nicholas' parents. He didn't know what that meant for them romantically, but right now he needed a teammate—a partner to help him with the decision. Doing it alone felt impossible. Doing it with Charlotte still felt impossible, albeit a little less scary.

When he emerged from the gardens and went to Le Soleil to find Charlotte, he was worried when the doorman told him she had just left hours earlier and not yet returned. When he asked to call up, the concierge declined, saying that they had guests. His own phone was dead. In all the fuss, he had completely forgotten to charge it.

Wracking his mind, Freddie tried to think of where Charlotte would go in a moment of crisis. Immediately, he thought back to ten years ago—she had left without saying a word. She had done it then, she could do it again.

Glancing at his watch, he mentally calculated the time he had. Monaco didn't have an airport. If she was leaving Monaco and returning to New York City, surely she would be heading to the Nice Côte d'Azur airport. It would be tight timing, but he was a former Formula One driver. He may be retired, but he wasn't out of the race yet. Surely he could make it there in no time.

TWENTY-FIVE

Charlotte

It turned out that tracking down Freddie and Nicholas proved harder than Charlotte anticipated. Freddie wasn't picking up his cell phone—no surprise there. He wasn't at the apartment, she had checked. She even went to the go-karting track, on the off chance that they had gone before Nicholas' arm was healed. No sign of them. She wandered around in circles through the meticulous winding streets, clocking in well over her goal of ten thousand steps per day.

Figuring that she should head back to see how her mémé and Violet were faring, she popped back into Le Soleil. The concierge stopped her on her way to the elevator.

"There was a man here to see you," they said. "Freddie Ridgeport. That Formula One racer. I told him you weren't here."

Charlotte drew in a breath, feeling her heart inflate with her lungs. "Where did he go?"

The concierge shrugged. "I don't know, *madame*. But when he left, he was muttering something about the airport."

Either Freddie was thinking of taking off himself, or he was trying to chase her down, thinking that she had gotten on a plane herself. She needed to find out. She found herself in the back of a taxi, racing to the airport. Until they hit Riviera traffic.

"Aren't there any back routes you can take?" Charlotte pleaded to the taxi driver.

The taxi driver shrugged and muttered something about *c'est la vie*.

Tapping her nails against one another, she tried counting her breaths one at a time. The last time she was in a taxi, she had been arriving in Monaco at a leisurely pace, no rush, to see her mémé who she had wrongfully thought needed her help. She had yet to meet someone more independent than Marguerite Levant and she should have known it. Now, she was racing off to see if Freddie was trying to track her down. It was a leap of faith, but she couldn't discount the possibility that he still cared for her. After all, he had only just proposed a short while earlier.

The taxi driver scoffed. "You see here? Hot heads. These guys, they think they own the roads."

Charlotte looked out of the window. On the side of the road was Freddie's Ferrari—she couldn't forget it. It appeared it was rear-ended. An SUV was parked behind it on the side of the highway blocking traffic, blinkers on. Her heart raced as she scanned the scene for Freddie, but it looked like everyone involved was gone, leaving only the tow trucks.

"Turn around," Charlotte nearly shouted.

"What? You want me to make a U-turn?" the driver joked. "I can't go anywhere right now."

Charlotte was stuck for the next half hour in traffic before the driver was able to get off at the next exit and drop her back in Monaco. She hadn't the slightest idea where Freddie was at this point and now it was dark.

"*Merci*," she said, tipping the driver and thanking him for his troubles.

Now, she had to check on her mémé and see how Violet was doing. It had only been one day, but it felt like a decade. Wearily, she made her way back up home. Home. It certainly had its problems.

Although on the outside, it was deceptively immaculate. Nothing was neat, clean, tidy, or organized in her personal life in the slightest. Taking a deep breath, she held her chin high. She could only handle so much at once. She was just one person. She would take it one step at a time and one mess at a time.

Upstairs, Violet was snoring softly on the couch.

"She hasn't moved one bit," her mémé said, her face lit up in excitement. "It's quite exciting, isn't it? She's a bit like a child. You know, you once got into some alcohol too young as well, you know. You slept it off for close to twelve hours."

Charlotte smiled, grateful to have had her mémé there to protect her. Her mémé hadn't asked how the mission to find Freddie had gone—it was probably written all over her face.

"Those were the days," Charlotte said, laughing in reminiscence.

"You need to get some sleep too, *non*?" her mémé asked with concern.

She nodded. There were times to fight and times to rest. It was nearing eleven in the evening. Nicholas would be asleep. Freddie would be inevitably home now and dealing with the insurance company. This wasn't the time. Besides, she didn't really know if he was even chasing her down to begin with.

Feeling deflated and exhausted, her pride slightly wounded, Charlotte gave her mémé a kiss before turning out the light. Tomorrow was another day.

How could she hope to be forgiven herself if she couldn't forgive the person right in front of her? Violet was already awake, sitting up on the sofa and massaging one of her temples with one hand. She held a cup of coffee in the other.

"I'm so sorry about last night," Violet whispered. "Gosh, what a mess."

Charlotte wasn't sure if it was the hangover or her guilt that made her sound so pitiful. Either way, she had decided to sit across from Violet and hear her out.

"How are you feeling?" Charlotte asked.

Violet winced. "I've felt better. Then again, I've also felt worse."

Charlotte couldn't help but laugh. She filled her own coffee and sat across from Violet.

"So what was last night all about?" Charlotte asked carefully.

Violet set down her coffee cup. "It's a bit of a crazy story. Are you sure you want to hear it?"

"I'm sure."

Taking a deep inhale, Violet began. She told the whole story of her passion for racing, meeting and falling for Freddie, her precarious financial situation, working with Randy and selling information, not meaning to hurt Freddie with those headlines, meeting Yanic, and finally making up one last, crazy story to sell to Randy.

"Since it's my last story that I'm selling to him, my credibility doesn't matter much anymore. I was going to sell him a made-up, crazy article about Freddie and you and your 'secret child'," she said using air quotes. "And because it's such a headline grabber, I would make a lot of money from it, but it would be easy to dispel. I know it doesn't sound like it as I say it aloud, but in my mind it was a win-win. A win for me because I get to make a lot of money and a win for Freddie since he could easily dispel the article."

Charlotte stared at Violet with an unreadable expression. "Right," she finally managed.

"I've been in such a dark space," Violet continued. "I don't know what's wrong with me. First I ruined the relationship with Freddie, then I dove into another relationship that I knew wasn't the right one for me. I swear I've been spiraling for a while. Sometimes things feel so out of control. I—I'm really sorry you got dragged into it. You and Freddie. Neither of you deserved it. Plus, that kid. He didn't deserve it either. Nicholas, is it?"

Charlotte nodded. "That's right."

"Just to confirm, Charlotte, I didn't sell the story," Violet said again. She showed Charlotte the text message exchange that she had with Randy.

Charlotte felt an ounce of relief. "You have no idea how glad I am you didn't sell that story," she said to Violet.

Violet sighed. "Me too. I guess I'll have to figure things out money-wise another way."

"Didn't you mention you love racing?" Charlotte asked. "Why don't you do something in that sphere?"

Violet laughed sadly. "I think that ship has sailed. I might have burned those bridges. But thanks for the suggestion. Don't worry about me, I'll figure something out. I always do."

"Well, you never know," Charlotte added hopefully.

"Thanks for taking me in last night," Violet said. "I must have been a real mess."

Charlotte shrugged. "Of course."

Violet pulled her legs up to her chest, wrapping them in her arms. "Gosh, I'm just sorry," she said, shaking her head in disbelief. "I mean, you definitely don't need to be sitting with me here today, helping me. Especially with all that I've done."

Charlotte felt a little hesitant to accept the words into her heart, but she smiled anyway. "Thank you, Violet. You deserve better for yourself." She realized as the words escaped her lips that she really meant it.

Violet looked up from where she had been fixing her gaze. "You know, I felt so mad that you were with Freddie at first. I guess it just brought up all that… emotion," she said vaguely. "But you're wonderful," she said with an incredulous laugh. "I can't believe I put all that stuff into his mind about Nicholas. I—I'm really sorry about that."

"Why did you do that, exactly?"

Violet shrunk into her seat, as if a cloud of shame had engulfed her. "I don't know. I guess I just needed to see it in his eyes that it wasn't true. He certainly confirmed it. But I didn't know it was going to make such a mess of things." She looked down before adding: "Sorry, I heard you and your grandmother talking earlier. It sounds like I put you in a really tough spot."

Charlotte nodded. "Yup, it certainly did."

Violet pulled a face. "I'm really sorry. You've been so nice to me. I've been really awful," Violet continued. "Is there anything I can do to make up for it?"

Charlotte thought for a minute. There was nothing that Violet could do for her or for Freddie—in fact, the best thing was probably for Violet to stay as far away from them as possible. Right now, she just felt grateful that Violet still seemed to have no idea that everything she had made up was true. Her ridiculous lie was totally, one-hundred percent true. Thank goodness she had no clue. One day, she presumed that Violet would learn that. A part of her still felt angry with Violet for stirring the pot as she had. But that didn't stop her heart from softening as she saw Violet across from her, looking desperate for any kind of advice.

"Well, for starters," Charlotte began. "I might recommend telling your fiancé that you either need some serious couples counseling or that it's probably not the right relationship."

Violet paused. Perhaps she was letting Charlotte's words sink in. "If I were to say anything to him, what would you recommend?"

"The truth," Charlotte said with conviction. "Just tell him the truth. For better or for worse, no matter his reaction, you'll never be left wondering 'what if' so long as you tell the truth. You'll never have a bitter hole in your heart, eating you up at night, so long as you tell the truth. It won't be easy, I'll tell you that much, but speaking from experience, it's the only thing that allows you to really move forward with your life. So either way, figure out what that means to you. That's what you can do."

One day, perhaps the whole world would know the truth about her own situation with Freddie and Nicholas. When it came to delicate matters, timing was everything. Before anyone else knew anything, she was going to have to get in touch with Freddie.

Violet wrinkled her nose. "The truth does all that?"

Charlotte smiled. "It does a whole lot more, Violet."

TWENTY-SIX

Violet

Violet had certainly made a mess of things, especially her relationship with her fiancé, her friendships, and even her connections to perfectly nice strangers, like Marguerite and Charlotte Levant. *Was someone still a stranger if you had slept on their couch and drank their coffee in the morning?* She hoped not.

Violet walked back from Le Soleil with a headache, shame flooding her twice as forcefully as the waves that lapped at the shoreline. The sun beating down on her made everything feel worse, especially the headache. She wished she hadn't worn those stupid high heels she knew would give her blisters, but they made her legs look so long and model-like. Now, she had to work not to limp as she cautiously put one foot in front of the other. Only a few more blocks until she arrived home.

She didn't bother calling a taxi since the streets were so busy and it would have meant more time waiting at Le Soleil, which she had felt desperate to get out of, not for lack of hospitality, but more due to her own feelings of regret.

Another pang of embarrassment hit as another memory resurfaced from the night before. She still remembered the evening she had but the details were fuzzy. Had she been standing on that corner the night before, accosting Charlotte? How *mortifying*.

She managed to get her way to her own Monaco apartment, which she had recently renovated to be entirely minimalist and contemporary. Her goal had been to be featured in the magazine Riviera Homes, but the editors hadn't even gotten back to her. She threw her keys onto the bare blonde-wood kitchen table and sat down on her Eames chair, burying her head in her hands. Was she all out of Tylenol? She certainly hoped not.

A knock on her door startled her. She wasn't expecting company. She certainly didn't want anyone else seeing her the way she was. On her tiptoes, she crept to her room, hoping to avoid making any noises.

The knocking became harder. Who on Earth could it be? Carefully looking through the peephole, her heart sank.

"Hey babe, I'm not feeling so good," she called out, leaning against the door for support. "I don't want you to catch whatever I've got," she fibbed, crossing her fingers behind her back.

"Come on, I'm sure it's not that bad," her fiancé, Yanic Blitzgrav said convincingly. "We're supposed to be married in a few days and I'm leaving for my bachelor's party soon. I wanted to say goodbye. Besides, I wanted to hear how your big night went."

A stab of fear struck her right at her core. She couldn't confess to him what had actually happened the night before. And she promised herself on the way home from Le Soleil that there would be no more lies… at least no more *big* ones. A little white lie in this case was just fine, she told herself. Besides, she hadn't even showered.

"No, I'm really feeling icky," she said, playing for time. "You go and enjoy your bachelor party. I'll be fine."

"You sure? Okay then…" Yanic said.

It had always been easy to fool Yanic, Violet thought, after saying goodbye to him and seeing him walk away through the peephole. She felt a smidgeon of… what was that feeling? Guilt? Shame? Embarrassment? Whatever it was, it felt so uncomfortable that she took a seat on the couch, her shoulders shaking as she tried to hold in the tears threatening to cascade down her cheeks.

What was going on? Violet certainly didn't know.

Taking out her phone to distract herself, she flipped through photos of her at her bachelorette party from the night before, cringing slightly. There were earlier photos on her phone of her, Yanic, and Yanic's son, Pierre. Him and Pierre looked genuinely happy. Violet felt a twinge in her chest, making it hard to breathe. She was supposed to be a wife and step-mother within the next few days. Instead of mentally preparing herself, she was trying to sabotage her ex and his new relationship in exchange for what? Enough money for rent? Suddenly there didn't seem to be enough money in the world for what she had done.

"What kind of a person does that?" she muttered aloud, fighting the urge to throw her phone across the room.

Her phone beeped. It was a text message from Randolph.

Any news on Freddie???

Violet stared at that text message with horror. A few days ago, perhaps even the day before, she would have responded very differently than she planned on now. Charlotte had been such an angel to her. Finally, she could send back a text message with the truth. Carefully, she typed back:

No story there. Sorry.

Pressing send, she felt a weight lifting off of her chest. This was where it ended. She wasn't going to play her dirty games anymore. Not with Freddie, not with Yanic. Perhaps this was the fresh start she had needed. A chance to make amends, none of it public, but instead more privately within her own mind.

She needed to sort things out with Yanic. He didn't deserve a wife who was only one-foot in the relationship. Maybe Charlotte was right: the truth could do a whole lot more than she thought. But only when used for the good, she would have added.

There were a lot of items in that apartment she could easily sell off. She didn't have to take any drastic action by being a mole anymore. This was going to be a new start. She sat back on her sofa. What on

Earth would that look like? Perhaps she would be a reporter? Or a journalist? She certainly had a knack for finding and weaving the threads of stories together. She liked the sound of that: Violet Macintyre, Formula One journalist. It certainly had the right ring to it. And maybe that ring made more sense to her than the one on her finger. Feeling clearer than she had in a very long time, Violet smiled. There was a lot of mess to clean up, but she could handle it. This was going to be her brand-new fresh start.

TWENTY-SEVEN

Freddie

Freddie hadn't slept all night. His entire life was blowing up in front of him. And yet, there was a sense of calm and serenity that had come over him. Perhaps it had something to do with learning he had a biological child he was finally reunited with. Perhaps it had to do with his precious Ferrari being rear-ended the evening before by someone on their phone. Luckily he had given himself tons of space ahead of him, so no one else was involved. The damage was minor, according to his assessment, but due to the serious cost of the car and the meticulous care he took of it, he didn't want to leave anything to chance. The damage was being appraised and he still needed to call the insurance company. But not even an accident to his precious car could overshadow the weight of what he had learned earlier that day.

If this had happened a month earlier, Freddie could only imagine the wrath the other poor driver would have had to endure. He could be quite the hothead. Now, he didn't have the energy for that. He had bigger things to focus on. Stuff of real importance. For the first time in his life, he felt he was racing towards his future, not running from his past.

Over the night, he had fretfully imagined all of the worst-case scenarios—perhaps he wasn't actually the father, and if he told Nicholas, it would create such psychological damage he may never recover. Then there was the possibility that Nicholas would react poorly regardless of the actual paternity. And what would Charlotte's role be going forward?

After dwelling and stewing on each possible scenario, he was fairly certain that he knew the outcome he wanted: he wanted to mend things with Charlotte. Certainly, a good couple's counselor might come into play to help them resolve some of the trust issues that inevitably would arise. But Charlotte had been eighteen, scared, and acting out of love for him and ultimately their child. Nicholas had a wonderful upbringing by two fantastic, doting parents. Perhaps if Nicholas was adopted by cruel, cold parents, he wouldn't have felt so willing to dig deep within himself and find forgiveness. Didn't everyone deserve a second chance?

Truthfully, Charlotte had been on his mind for ten years. Losing her again made the impossible situation seem even more unmanageable. With her by his side, somehow it felt easier to breathe.

A knock came from his door. "Come in," he called.

Nicholas opened the door and was rubbing the sleep from his eyes. "When can we get to the track?" he asked, stifling a yawn.

Freddie couldn't help but laugh. "Kiddo, you just got your cast off. How's your arm feeling?"

Nicholas rotated his shoulder carefully, looking serious. "It feels a bit stiff, but the doctor told me that was to be expected."

Freddie nodded. "I'll tell you what—why don't we go to the car show today? I know it's not the same as racing, but they'll have some pretty amazing cars on display. Who knows, you might even see some famous racers."

Nicholas smiled. "You're my favorite race car driver," he said. "Hey, can you make crêpes? I'm starving."

"Your favorite, huh? Even more than Christian Driver?"

Nicholas mulled over the question. "Well, at least equal."

Freddie gave a silent whoop and couldn't wait to rub

Christian's nose in it. Equal! That was much better than Christian winning by a long shot. Freddie also knew that Nicholas had a keen desire for crêpes and there was a certain brilliance to children, knowing how to say just the right thing before making a request. Freddie wouldn't have rather done anything else in the world than eat breakfast with his son... except Nicholas still didn't know that bit. "Sure, why don't you get the table set?"

His crêpes were a little lumpy, not perfectly circular, but it didn't seem to matter to Nicholas. He thought that his dad-skills were coming along quite nicely, although they could still use a bit of fine-tuning.

With dark circles under his eyes and emotions fuelled by coffee and adrenaline, he knew that he needed to find Charlotte. Last night had been a colossal failure. Perhaps just like their relationship, that first attempt had all the right intention, but it wasn't the right timing and an accident had occurred. Now, it was time for take two.

Take two would have to wait until after the car show, of course. With Freddie, parenting came first. A certain instinct had taken over. He wouldn't have recognized himself a few months earlier. Now, he was at a car show early on a Sunday morning with his nine-year-old son. It was a far cry from his old life where Sundays were for recovering from Friday and Saturday nights. The car show was filled with eager faces, Nicholas' included. Freddie had never been outside of the Monte-Carlo Casino this early. He was surprised by how pleasant it was—cars, scenery, and his son.

"Wow, look at that one!" Nicholas pointed out one car after another, seemingly more impressed by the second.

Freddie wondered how he hadn't clued into this being his son earlier. He had been exactly the same at his age.

"So, tell me more about this Miranda girl you're so interested in," Freddie said, hoping to learn a little bit more about Nicholas' life.

Nicholas looked equally pleased to be asked and sorry with his response. "She's the smartest girl at school. Everyone knows it. Plus, she's really nice. She never teases this one girl in our class who all the other girls make fun of. I know Miranda doesn't really like this other girl, but she'll still have lunch with her because that girl doesn't have other friends. But everyone loves Miranda. Including the boys."

Freddie smiled. "She sounds pretty great. Have you talked to her?"

Nicholas nodded. "Yeah, a few times. She came up to me to tell me how sorry she was when my parents died."

"How did that go?"

Nicholas shrugged. "It went okay. I didn't really feel like talking about it at the time."

Freddie put a hand on Nicholas' shoulder. "I get the feeling she understood."

Nicholas smiled before his face burst into joy. "It's her. Over there, look!"

Freddie followed where Nicholas was pointing. A brown-haired girl with two adults were examining an acid green car. "Why don't you go talk to her?" Freddie suggested.

Nicholas seemed to seize up in fear.

"Come on," Freddie continued. "You just recovered from a racing injury. That's the stuff hero's are made of."

Nicholas laughed nervously. "Are you sure?"

"Come on, what do you have to lose?"

Freddie had to practically step on Nicholas' toes, but eventually he convinced him to walk up to Miranda. She was with two well-dressed men, both appearing to be in their forties. One of them seemed to recognize Freddie before Nicholas had a chance to speak.

"Chris, look," the man said as they approached, poking the other man on his shoulder. "It's Freddie Ridgeport."

The man who seemed to be Chris took off his sunglasses and broke into a smile. "Freddie Ridgeport! We're big fans."

Nicholas looked up at Freddie with a quizzical expression.

Freddie smiled. "I'm guessing you guys are into Formula One? If you weren't, I guess that would be a bit weird."

The two men laughed and introduced themselves as Chris and Kyle, Miranda's parents and *major* Formula One fans. In fact, one of Miranda's parents had worked in Formula One's traveling circus, as they liked to call it, for many years himself. As Freddie made conversation with them, he was aware of Miranda smiling at Nicholas, who looked like he had just seen a ghost. It took all of his might not to laugh.

"And this is my, uh, well, this is Nicholas," Freddie managed, as he introduced the kid.

Shyly, Nicholas smiled at Miranda and up at Miranda's parents. "It's very nice to see you again, Miranda, and nice to meet the two of you," he said confidently. "When I grow up, I'm going to be a Formula One driver too. Just like Freddie."

Chris and Kyle beamed. "I'm sure you will, Nicholas. Which of these cars is your favorite?"

"I like this green one," Nicholas said thoughtfully as he pointed to an exotic car. "It reminds me of the go-kart I raced in for the first time."

Miranda looked curious. "You raced?"

Nicholas nodded. "Yeah, it was pretty cool. Maybe you can come with me sometime."

"Would the two of you like to join us? We'd love the company. Wouldn't we, Miranda?" Chris asked.

Miranda wasn't paying attention. She was examining another nearby parked racecar with Nicholas, who seemed to have gotten a surge of confidence.

Freddie was learning so much about Nicholas already—like how he seemed so unsure of himself and doubted his ability to do the things he wanted, but when he eventually got into the situation, he was a star.

"Well, I think I can speak for Nicholas in saying that he would be delighted."

"Amazing. Because Miranda has been talking about Nicholas non-stop. She keeps talking about what a kind boy he is. How even after everything he has gone through, he has been volunteering at his lunch-break to help tutor some of the other students in math who aren't picking it up as quickly," Kyle said with admiration.

Freddie's heart melted. "He is?"

"You're doing a great job with him," Chris put in. "Seriously, he seems like such a sweet kid."

"Well, I can say the same about Miranda. Freddie's talked about her nonstop," he said, before checking his watch. "I'd love to spend more time with you guys, but I have something I need to do that is a little time sensitive. Would it be alright if Nicholas toured the rest of the car show with you?"

"Of course! Yes, go. As a single dad, I can imagine it's hard getting a minute to yourself," Kyle agreed.

Freddie thanked the two of them profusely, ran the idea by Nicholas who agreed with a huge grin, and exchanged phone numbers with Chris and Kyle, agreeing to set up another play-date for the two of them soon.

As Freddie left the car show, he felt equally grateful for the time he had and also strangely sad to be leaving Nicholas. He would have loved to see that car show with him. But he also knew that Nicholas would be fine without him. He needed to let the kid spread his wings. Plus, he had an important mission right now, one that would hopefully benefit both him and Nicholas down the line. He didn't want to wait another second for it.

Freddie left Nicholas at the car show with Miranda and her parents, which would buy him at least an hour to try and find Charlotte. With his recharged phone, he sent Charlotte a text message, telling her he wanted to see her. No response.

He wandered through the Jardins Saint-Martin again—this time, the bright afternoon light and dry heat made every muscle in his body relax. It was tough to feel too stressed looking out at the Mediterranean from a world-class garden. All around him, cacti and palm trees thrived alongside the rocky cliffs leading to the coast.

His phone buzzed. Charlotte had replied. His heart skipped a beat as he opened the message.

Turn around, it read.

Slowly, Freddie swiveled to face the opposite direction. Standing in front of him was Charlotte, holding her own phone in her hand.

Cautiously, Freddie took one step towards her. He was half delirious from sleep deprivation, but to him she seemed like an angel.

Charlotte stepped closer to him also, until the two of them were so close that he could feel the heat from her body on his.

"Hi," he said quietly.

She looked up at him and smiled sweetly. "Hi," she replied back with a grin. "I was on my way to the car show. I figured you and Nicholas would probably be there."

Freddie felt the deep yearning to kiss her. The warm scent of her perfume reminded him of simpler times. Before he had a chance to gather his thoughts, Charlotte stood up on her tippy-toes, meeting his lips with hers. He was twenty years old again. It felt just like old times—the second time around.

Magic. He pulled away momentarily, searching her clear eyes with his. He wasn't sure what he was looking for, but he found it. His heart swelled and something inside of him healed. She gave a small smile, hints of sadness and love and longing evident in her eyes. There was something mysterious about Charlotte, something about her that he felt he could never quite figure out. Perhaps it was what she had been hiding that had put up a veil. For whatever reason, today he felt he understood her with crystal clarity, as if he could read every emotion that came up.

Reaching into his pocket, Freddie took out a small box and got down on one knee. His heart was pounding. From Charlotte's expression, this was already off to a better start than the last time. Perhaps the two of them just needed another second chance at this, too.

"Charlotte," Freddie began. "Charlotte..."

"Yes!" she burst out, before he had even had the chance to say the words. She clamped her hands over her mouth, eyes wide with delighted excitement. "I mean, go on..."

Freddie laughed, his heart feeling light and fluttery. This was it. This was his moment. The moment he had been waiting for the last ten years. He wanted to ask it then, and he had wished he had the opportunity to ask it every day since. Heart thudding, palms sweating, and he had never felt more certain about anything before in his life.

"Will you marry me?"

Charlotte nodded slowly as tears filled in her eyes as he opened up the ring box. Carefully, he placed the engagement ring on her finger. It fit perfectly.

"Now we can be a family," Charlotte said, tears streaming down her cheeks.

Freddie wrapped her in his arms, feeling like all of those fragmented pieces of his life were finally coming together. It was all finally making sense.

"We've gotten lucky with this second chance," Freddie said, kissing his fiancé. "All thanks to you."

Charlotte shook her head and smiled, her eyes sparkling with tears and joy. "No, all thanks to Nicholas."

TWENTY-EIGHT

Marguerite

Oh, how Marguerite loved happy endings. She clasped her hands together in delight as Charlotte showed off her sparkling diamond ring. It shone almost as brightly as her granddaughter, who was smiling from ear to ear.

"My dear," she muttered again, tears springing to her eyes. "You have no idea how overjoyed this makes me. To see you so happy…" she trailed off again. Ever since Charlotte had told her the wonderful news, she had been so delightedly taken aback that she hadn't been able to string a sentence together.

"You think *you're* happy?" she asked with overflowing enthusiasm. "I have never felt so good in my life. Never ever. Never ever *ever*. And not just the proposal, that's all fine and wonderful, but it's what it represents. Me, Freddie, and Nicholas all together."

Marguerite's heart skipped a beat. She held up her cup of tea, which she enjoyed on her balcony when Charlotte popped by and sprang the news on her. With trembling hands she took a careful sip, daring herself to ask the question that had been building in her for weeks.

"So, does that mean that I'll get to meet young Nicholas then?" Her voice sounded so unsure in that moment, with almost a birdlike quality to it.

Charlotte locked eyes with her, looking suddenly serious. "Yes. And he cannot wait to meet you."

Marguerite had wished for this moment herself for the last decade. It hadn't only been Charlotte who had suffered. Years of regret, guilt, and uncertainty were slowly unraveling in her, loosening the knots they had tied around her heart.

"Well," she managed in a strangled voice. "That would be wonderful."

'Wonderful' was putting it lightly. But she didn't want to put too much pressure on the situation. After all, that young boy had gone through an awful lot. Another concern popped into her mind. She had spent years avoiding Freddie Ridgeport when he had been right under her nose. She could only imagine what he thought of her.

"And Freddie?"

Charlotte cleared her throat. "I explained everything to him. He fully understands. He is really looking forward to catching up with you."

Another knot loosened its grip from somewhere deep inside.

"Well, that's a relief," she said. "It could have been quite awkward."

A trill of laughter erupted between them. After all these years, who could have predicted things would have ever turned out the way that they did? Certainly she never would have put her money on it. Life had this miraculous ability to surprise her, even when she thought that life had thrown all of the surprises her way. Now, the greatest gift she could have received, of getting to meet her grandson, was coming at the perfect time.

She stood up, this time without her walker or cane. Charlotte looked on admiringly as she did a little twirl. "Not bad?" she asked, jutting out her hip, which twinged slightly as she did so. She would have to be careful not to overdo it.

"Just perfect," Charlotte said with a smile. "Do you want to meet him now?"

Her heart sped up. "Now?"

Charlotte nodded. "Mhm. He's downstairs at this lovely patisserie grabbing some macarons."

"Well, I don't know if *now* is the time," she said, feeling suddenly flustered and flushed. She wasn't ready. She hadn't prepared herself to meet her grandson right now. There was so much planning that could be done… the perfect meal, the perfect drinks…

"Come on," Charlotte said gently. "There's no time like the present. It's never going to be perfect. We might as well give it our best shot. It seems to have worked out okay for me. Plus, he's dying to meet you."

Her eyes lit up. "Really? He's dying to meet me?"

Charlotte nodded. "He certainly is. I've told him all about you."

Marguerite would have to pretend that she hadn't secretly been keeping an eye on that beautiful boy all of those years. Of course, she had distanced herself from the Stefanos after they had legally adopted him. She couldn't bear the pain and anguish it caused her not to be his grandmother. Instead, she had surreptitiously watched from afar, seeing him at *La Marche de la Condamine* or the *Place des Arms* with his parents. It seemed to be an unwritten rule that she always turned the other way, but watchfully kept one eye on him. How she had longed to go up and say *Bonjour*. But now she had a chance. That one chance she had been waiting for over the last decade. Now was as good a time as ever.

"All right," Marguerite said, with only a slight tremble to her voice. She held her chin up and walked to the painted white armoire. Inside, she carefully took out a photograph from the day that Nicholas was born. The nurse had taken it while she cradled the sweet baby in her arms, Charlotte watching from the bed. She placed the photograph on the marble mantelpiece. Now she could bring it out. Now she could display it. Now she could finally be the grandmother she had always wanted to be. "Let's do this," she said, grabbing her purse and walking towards the door. There was no time like the present and she was going to soak up every second that she had.

What a gift, to be given a second chance. Marguerite held that thought close to her heart as she stepped out the door with Charlotte in tow, hardly believing that she was finally heading to meet her grandson. What a magical, magnificent, painful, and humbling gift.

TWENTY-NINE

Charlotte

Charlotte could barely believe she had been engaged for an entire month. Her sparkling engagement ring was a part of her. She felt naked whenever she forgot to put it on. And it felt like years earlier that she had returned home to Monaco. So much had changed. Her mémé was healed from her fall and now making trips to the market on her own, but Charlotte still accompanied her most of the time. Nicholas was healed from his shoulder injury and had his second go-kart race coming up—he had already won his first by quite a bit. She had moved into Freddie's apartment and now lived with her fiancé and son. That was undoubtedly the biggest shift—having Nicholas fully aware of the situation and for the first time in her life, to have this huge secret out in the open.

Telling Nicholas the truth was the scariest thing she had ever done. It had made her even more concerned than when she told Freddie. At least she had Freddie by her side. Before they had spoken with Nicholas, the two of them had consulted with a family therapist about the best way to move forward and what language to use. They even agreed to continue with family therapy for a few sessions just the two of them, to work through the lingering effects of what was left unsaid for ten years.

When the two of them sat Nicholas down to discuss the truth, Charlotte's heart had pounded so hard she thought she might have a heart attack. Somehow, they had managed to get through it. There were many tears, on her end and even a few from Freddie. But Nicholas had sat there still, a serene expression, taking it all in. It scared Charlotte how calm he was. Only after everything was put out there did she understand. Once they were done, the two of them waited in pained silence for Nicholas' response. It was agony waiting to see how he reacted.

"I learned about eye color in biology last year," Nicholas had said, as she and Freddie listened in stunned silence.

Charlotte had wondered if Nicholas had even been paying attention to what they had said. She certainly didn't want to go over it all again—her courage was already depleted after the adrenaline rush of telling Nicholas the truth.

Nicholas had continued. "I have brown eyes. But my parents, Roland and Isabelle, both had blue eyes. Do you know what percentage chance there is for two blue eyed parents to have a brown eyed child?"

Charlotte and Freddie both shook their heads.

"Zero," Nicholas said. "Zero percent chance. Then I started asking to see pictures of my birth—they had a lot of pictures of me as an infant, but none from the hospital or anything like that. It took me a little while to figure it out, but I knew I had to have been adopted. I never told my parents. It was clear that it wasn't something they wanted to discuss or bring up."

Charlotte held her breath. The three of them had discussed Nicholas' realization a year before Isabelle and Roland Stefano died in the car accident. They talked about Nicholas' upbringing and how wonderful the Stefanos were as his parents.

"We're not trying to replace anyone. No one will ever be able to replace Isabelle and Roland," Charlotte had told Nicholas, just like the therapist had recommended.

"I know that," Nicholas had said. "Besides, it's a bit of a relief to find out that I now know my biological parents. And that it's you two. I don't think I could have asked for anything better."

With those words, it was like Charlotte shed a ten thousand pound jacket she had worn for a whole decade. Ever since that conversation a few weeks earlier, Charlotte had existed as if she floated around on a cloud. Nothing got to her. Everything had worked out. It hadn't been easy and it had certainly been painful. But with the strength and courage to tell the truth, allowing that festering secret to dry up in the sunlight, she had learned that she could handle anything.

She had given up that phrase: keep it light and keep it shiny, then emotions will be tidy. It no longer served her. She wondered if it ever really did. Emotions were big, sometimes chaotic, and messy. Nothing in life was perfectly clean. It was always an illusion to help her feel in control of a situation that was entirely, one hundred percent outside of her control.

Somehow, everything had worked out despite the mess.

Nothing was tidy now. There were still a lot of lingering trust issues that both she and Freddie would inevitably have to work through. But at least they had agreed they would work on it together.

The wedding hadn't had much planned as of yet. As she fussed with the table setting one evening before dinner—she had salmon baking in the oven for a sunset dinner—Nicholas came up to her.

"I have one stipulation about the two of you getting married," he said.

Charlotte stood up a little straighter. "Oh yeah? What's that?" she asked, a small ripple of fear running through her.

Nicholas smiled proudly. "I want to walk you down the aisle."

Charlotte could have melted right there and then. There had been so many tenderhearted moments in the past few weeks; it was hard to get through the day without feeling overwhelming gratitude.

"As long as we get married at the end of the day, you can slip-and-slide down the aisle," Freddie teased as he stepped onto the deck, barefoot. He had just gotten back from a successful day scuba diving with Christian and had even brought Nicholas along with him on the boat. Nicholas had snorkeled and had proclaimed that it was one of the best days of his life when he had arrived home.

"Nicholas just suggested walking me down the aisle," Charlotte gushed.

Freddie nodded and smiled. "I think that sounds perfect."

"After all," Nicholas began. "I want to make a good impression for Miranda. She'll be in the second row. She said that to sit in the first row, as I had suggested, would be rude."

Charlotte kneeled down and gave Nicholas a kiss on his cheek. "She can sit wherever she likes. This isn't going to be a big wedding. Nice and small."

"As long as the three of us are together forever, I don't care where we get married or how many people are there," Freddie said.

"Promise?" Nicholas asked, a small quiver in his voice. "Promise we'll be together, the three of us, forever?

"It's a promise," Charlotte agreed.

"It's a promise," Freddie echoed.

Charlotte's heart felt full. Three promises. One family. All together forever. They weren't promising each other perfection. Charlotte didn't want that, anyway. She wanted a real life. And miraculously, life was now a series of green lights. To Charlotte, it was proof that truth towered over secrets, broken hearts could heal, and that forgiveness—that beautiful act of forgiveness—could result in the richest, most delicious life. She was proof. And she was enjoying every second of it... well, most seconds of it. Sometimes the truth just plain hurt and there was no getting around it. But she could handle it and there wasn't a moment she was going to waste.

"Come on," she said. "Let's head to the race track. I hear that there's an up and coming star in the racing world."

Nicholas beamed. "Right behind you."

Freddie grabbed the items off of the table and put them away. "We should grab Marguerite along the way."

"I can't wait for her to see me race." Nicholas said.

"Come on, team. Let's go!" Charlotte called out to the two of them.

The three of them left the apartment, hand in hand, talking and laughing the whole way to MonacoGo. Charlotte smiled. This wasn't the life that she had ever hoped or expected for herself. This was so, so much better.

THIRTY

Nicholas

Ten years later

Nicholas breathed in the languid Monaco air on a warm July afternoon. His mother passed him a croissant, still warm from the oven, as the three of them sat on their balcony. His dad was already dressed, wearing a shirt with Nicholas' racing number on it: 62.

Nicholas had already given an interview to the press earlier that week about why he had chosen that number.

"I chose the first number, six, because that's the number of people in my family: me, my mom, my dad, my late adoptive parents, Isabelle and Roland Stefano, and my grandmother, Marguerite Levant. I chose the second number, two, because I've had a second chance to build my family and my life."

The interviewer, Violet Macintyre, had smiled. "What a beautiful answer. Thanks, Nicholas. We're looking forward to seeing how you race today. If it's anything like what we've seen earlier this season, I think we're in for a treat."

Nicholas had smiled politely and thanked the interviewer, as he came to be trained to do by the media team, before leaving to go off to the side. That entire week turned out to be packed with interviews, media and press appearances, and parties. It was exhilarating, exhausting, and the best time of his life. His mom and dad had watched every single one of his races from the sidelines with eager smiles the whole way.

His dad passed him a cup of espresso, putting on his sunglasses to shield himself from the bright morning light. "We couldn't be more proud of you, Nicholas," Freddie said to him for what felt like the millionth time. "You've not only gotten one of the twenty seats in Formula One, which is such an accomplishment in itself, but you're fighting for first place this season so far. I mean, everyone expected you to do well, but I don't think anyone expected *this*."

His mom shook her head in disbelief. "I mean, you've been working so hard for the last few years. Well, since you got started racing. And your driving shows it. We always knew you could make it to Formula One and be one of the best drivers on the grid, but you've done it so *early*!"

Nicholas smiled shyly. "Thanks mom and dad," he muttered, feeling his cheeks becoming pink. Even after all of his success, he still never felt totally comfortable receiving so much praise. He supposed he had better get used to it.

"You've worked so hard," his dad continued. "I don't think you've taken much more than a few days off of practicing in a row since you were what? Nine?"

"Nine, that's right," his mother added, nodding her head.

It was true. For the last decade, a lot had changed in his life. One of the most notable, other than reuniting with his biological parents, was his steep ascent into the racing world after getting a seat on the Formula 4, later Formula 3, then Formula 2 team, before that incredible day when his dream was realized: he was officially had one of the coveted twenty seats on the Formula One track. His trajectory appeared similar to his dad's; of course, he was doing it all a little sooner than everyone had expected. Today would be his fifth race as an official F1 driver. There were twenty-three races total. He had either won or come in a close second for each race so far, which was unheard of for a rookie.

He sent a silent prayer to the sky, thanking his Ma and Father, who he often thought of and fondly remembered. From somewhere deep within, he felt they were helping guide him and perhaps throwing a little luck his way.

"I'm a little nervous," he admitted. "Racing in my hometown. So many people are counting on me." Although he had developed a reputation for being fearless on the track, he could only admit such things to his parents.

His dad smiled at him and clapped him on the shoulder. "You'd be crazy not to be, son."

His mom looked down at her left hand and smiled. "And just think. Your very first Monaco race happening on our anniversary. Ten years. My, how the time flies."

Nicholas could remember the day his parents got married with crystal clarity. It was a warm summer day, not dissimilar to this one. He was nine-years-old and chuffed to have been asked to be the best man. They had gotten married in a park overlooking the sea and his mom had worn a white dress with off-the-shoulder straps. Mostly, he remembered that at the reception, they had a chocolate fountain that he was given unlimited access to. It was funny the things that stuck in his memory. His crush at the time, Miranda, had come to the wedding accompanied by her dads. Who knew that crush would have turned into such a complicated, wonderful relationship?

"I've got to give Miranda a call," Nicholas said, looking down at his phone. Over the years, that girl had become his very best friend. She had been there at his first race. He had seen her through heartbreak as she navigated her on-again off-again relationship with Markus, who was back then and continued to remain a thorn in his side. He turned out to be too focused on racing to think about having a girlfriend. Well, perhaps he had thought about it a little more than he cared to admit. Although fear wasn't something that most people thought about when it came to Nicholas Stefano, there was one thing he felt absolutely terrified of. And he had never gotten the courage to tell Miranda how he felt.

Miranda was now involved in the Formula One world herself. She had made a name for herself as the must-have personal trainer and was working exclusively with his rival team. It wasn't exactly ideal.

He left the balcony, leaving his parents to talk amongst themselves, and went to his bedroom, carefully shutting the door. Even though he was nineteen, sometimes he still felt like that nine-year old who had just stepped into that apartment for the first time, hands nearly shaking. He held his phone in his hands, putting it on speakerphone, waiting to get through. He expected that she would be getting ready for race day. Perhaps she had a moment or two to spare.

"Hello?" came Miranda's giggling voice. There was someone in the background talking to her.

"Hey," he said, feeling his heart flutter in his chest. "How's it going?" For some reason, lately he had felt especially self-conscious whenever he talked on the phone with her.

"Stop it," she muttered in a whisper to whoever was in the background. Nicholas' heart sunk. "Okay, sorry, hi!" she said direction into the receiver. "Are you ready for your race?"

"I hope so," he said with a laugh. "Are you with someone?"

"Oh, just Markus," she said, a hint of awkwardness to her voice. "He, uh, surprised me here at the paddock."

Nicholas was an idiot. He should have greeted her in person. He could have surprised everyone by showing up to his rival team's paddock and sweeping her off of her feet. "Right," he managed. "Well—"

"—Have you done your routine?" Miranda asked, interrupting him. His heart softened. Typical Miranda. Even though she wanted her team to win, he knew a part of her was always rooting for him.

Nicholas laughed. "Not yet. But I will." Miranda was the one person, other than his parents and the team principal, who knew about his pre-race routine: gargle with mouthwash three times, take twenty deep breaths, and visualize the grid twice, winning once, and passing no one since he is at the front of the pack. In fact, she had helped him with it—a secret the two of them would tell *no one* since she was technically working for his rival.

"Well, I'll be thinking of you," she said. "Break a leg. And keep your wits about you. This isn't going to be an easy race."

Nicholas felt heat rising in his body. The two of them spoke the same language. They breathed the same passion. He could hear it in her voice, in her tone. He was exactly the same way.

"I can't wait," he said, meaning every word.

In the background, he could hear Markus saying something to Miranda in what sounded like a frustrated tone.

"I should go," Miranda said, a little too brightly. "But seriously, Nicholas. Good luck. And I'll be thinking about you. Whatever happens today."

Nicholas didn't want to jinx anything, but he was pretty sure he could feel it too. A tingling sensation all throughout his body. Like something amazing was just around the corner.

"It's bound to be interesting. I'll catch up with you after the race, okay?" he said, hoping Markus could hear him. "I'll take you out for dinner at that new seaside restaurant you like. What's it called again?"

Nicholas knew exactly the name of that restaurant. He had already made reservations, but he wanted to play it cool.

"Le Bernadin? Oh, Nicholas. That would be great. Okay, I've really got to go, but I'll be thinking of you."

Nicholas smiled. "Okay. Bye Miranda."

"Not bye," she said playfully. "See you later!"

He laughed. "Right. See you later."

He hung up, thinking that Miranda was one of those people who thought about the danger involved in car racing frequently. She reminded him more about the dangers of racing more than even he thought about it, and he was certainly not naive to the risks involved in the sport he loved. Earlier in the season, she had burst into tears when she saw him at the end of one of his races after he had a near crash with another driver.

Nicholas headed back to be with his parents. He needed to shift gears. He couldn't think about Miranda or the gnawing sensation inside of him that Markus was back in her life… *again.* Not that he was the jealous type. But it didn't help that he had secretly been in love with her since he had met her ten years earlier.

But he couldn't think about that. Today was race day. He had to get his game face on. Over the years, he had become an expert at compartmentalizing his life. When he needed to shift to racing, he had laser focus and nothing could distract him from the race.

"Everything all right?" his mom asked, a note of concern in her voice.

Nicholas forced a bright smile. "Great. She's doing well. She's really making a name for herself in the Formula One world."

"I meant with you, silly," his mom said with a laugh. "Of course we love Miranda, but she's coaching your biggest competitor. How are *you* feeling?"

Nicholas laughed. "I'm ready."

"I have no doubt," his dad said. "I mean, look at the kid? He's a natural. Plus, his mom is the most passionate driver out there. You've got genetics on your side," his dad teased. All of them knew that his mom hated driving but adored watching races.

"How is Gene? Is he recovered from his injury?"

Gene Stromball was his biggest rival and a three-time World Champion driver. Nicholas had hit the ground running when he got started, and had been Gene's only real competitor since his domination of the sport for the last three years. Today he had one main objective: to beat Gene. And Gene wanted to win more than anything. Luckily, so did Nicholas.

It was really too bad that Miranda was coaching him.

"Apparently his left thumb is fine," Nicholas said, citing what he had heard amongst his team. "The lesson seems to be: you shouldn't ride a horse during racing season if you've never tried it before."

"Well, use everything to your advantage," his dad said seriously. "Formula One demands that of you."

Nicholas nodded and checked his watch. "Right. Well, I should get going. I'll see you after the race, mom?"

His mother smiled. "For sure. I'll be there with mémé. She'll be waving to you, Nicholas. Make sure you send a wave in her direction!"

"I always do," he said with a smile. "Dad, you ready?"

To make an already ideal career even better, his dad was his manager. It certainly helped having a dad with a Formula One career like his had. Besides, Freddie had told him that retirement just wasn't his cup of tea. He needed something else to focus on. It turned out that he was an even better manager than he was a racer, and that was certainly saying a lot.

"Ready. Let's go, champ."

Racing had a way of captivating every ounce of his attention. His heart pounded in his chest. He had placed second in his qualifying lap, meaning that he started in second place on the grid. Gene was ahead of him.

One person popped up in his mind. Miranda. He certainly hoped that she was watching and *maybe* even secretly rooting for him to win. To him, that mattered almost as much as winning, which said a lot. Trying to shake thoughts of Miranda from his mind, he heard a voice come through his earpiece.

"Go win, kid," came his dad's voice.

Nicholas took a steadying breath. "Will do, dad."

He looked to the stands, where he knew his mom and grandmother were watching. Although they couldn't see him, he sent a nod in their direction and a silent prayer to his late adoptive parents.

This was it. Nicholas knew that he had already won in the lottery of life. Sure, there had been challenges, difficulties, and unconventional attributes about his upbringing. But knowing where it had all led him, he would never have it any other way. The lights began to blink, signaling that the race was about to start. Nicholas felt the familiar joy, excitement, exhilaration bubbling up in him and he pulled down his helmet.

3-2-1. The race was off.

"Woo hoo hoo hoo" he shouted to no one in particular, pressing his foot all the way down on the gas. One thing not everyone knew about racing Formula One cars: it was incredibly, seriously fun.

Nicholas navigated the twists and turns of the grid with precision. He listened to the voice in his ear. His speed, timing, and navigation of the grid was impeccable. Breaking at all the right points, accelerating when he needed to. The car was performing just as he needed it to.

"This is it. This is my time!" Nicholas cried out, with the finish line in sight as he managed his final lap. Gene was just behind him. He was in first place. This was almost it. The win was so close, he could nearly taste it.

As Nicholas flew through the finish line, cheers erupted from the fans.

He had won the Monaco Grand Prix. He had won the race! Nicholas screamed in relief and delight. His team ran to the track, waving and putting up one finger, signaling his podium finishing place. They were hugging and shouting at one another. It looked like a parade.

Tears welled in Nicholas' eyes as he pulled to a stop.

"This is it, son. You did it! You've won!" came his dad's voice through his earpiece.

Nicholas was shaking as he stood up, emerging from the car and raising his hands above his head. His team and the crowd roared their applause. It was the best feeling in the world.

"Thank you," Nicholas yelled to his team. "I couldn't have done it without all of you. This win is yours!" he said, pumping his fist in the air. His whole team shouted, hooting and hollering, and his dad came into view giving him the thumbs up, a giant smile plastered on his tanned face.

As his team embraced him and he shook millions of hands, adrenaline pumping through his veins, he looked up at the crowd and waved to his grandmother. He was sure she was watching with a keen eye, just as she always did.

A few girls came up to him, presumably family members of the team, asking for his autograph and pictures. Of course, he was obliged and delighted.

"You're my favorite racer," one of the girls said, clinging to the signed piece of paper like her life depended on it.

Nicholas smiled and gave them a wink before turning to meet his dad, the team principal, and head to the podium where he would stand in first place. He couldn't wait. He was Nicholas Stefano. And he planned on this being the first Monaco Grand Prix he would win of *many* races he intended to come in first. He flashed a grin while trying to memorize every second of that moment. After all, he was just getting started.

Buckle up.

The End

Acknowledgements

I want to thank **you**, dear reader, for picking up this book! I hope that you enjoyed it. I had a blast writing it.

Thank you, Jess, for your incredible edits and encouragement. I couldn't have done it without you.

I'd like to say a huge thank you to my husband, Ryan, and to my incredible family who are so supportive of my writing career.

And finally, I'd like to say a special thanks to Leo, my beautiful baby boy.

About the Author

KAYA QUINSEY HOLT is the author of MAYBE IN MONACO as well as several romance and women's fiction books. Her books have sold worldwide, have been translated into multiple languages, and adapted for audiobooks.

Head to Kaya's website (www.kayaquinsey.com) to be the first

to get sneak peaks and details about

A MONACO MINUTE, the second book in

Kaya Quinsey Holt's Monaco series.

Coming 2023.

www.kayaquinsey.com

@KayaQuinseyHolt

@KayaQuinseyHolt

@KayaQuinseyHolt

@KayaQuinseyHolt

Other Books by Kaya Quinsey Holt

The Marseille Millionaire

The Belles of Positano

Fate at the Wisteria Estate

A Date at the Wisteria Estate

Paris Mends Broken Hearts

A Coastal Christmas

Valentine in Venice

Printed in Great Britain
by Amazon

28492152R00126